Closet CONFESSION

KINDLE ALEXANDER

Closet Confession

Edited by Jae Ashley
Cover art by Reese Dante http://www.reesedante.com
Licensed material is used for illustrative purposes only and any person depicted in the licensed material is a model.

First Edition September 2015
Previously Published as part of the Night Shift Anthology
ISBN ebook: 978-1-941450-07-9

Published by: The Kindle Alexander Collection LLC

TRADEMARK ACKNOWLEDGEMENTS

The author acknowledges the trademarked status and trademark owners of the following trademarks mentioned in this work of fiction:

Band-Aid: Johnson & Johnson Corporation

Styrofoam: The Dow Chemical Company

DEDICATION

Perry, you are missed every day.

Kindle, you are forever in our hearts.

Denise Milano Sprung this is for you and your brother Keith. From almost the minute we met you, the two of you have held a special place in our hearts. I know he's incredibly proud of everything you've accomplished in his honor. I know I am.

Always big, giant hugs.

CHAPTER 1

Chaotic commotion in the Tulane Medical Emergency Room resonated with a familiar symphony in the background as Dr. Derek Babineaux tried to tune everything out. He was propped against a vacant countertop in a back corner of the nurses' station. He typed quickly, making notes into the chart of his last patient, hoping to move the paperwork along a little faster on such an incredibly busy night. He felt, more than heard, the stirrings behind him and reached over, quickly scribbling on a prescription pad that lay nearby, authorizing the needed medication for his patient.

"Here, Amanda." He never looked up from the screen as he slid the prescription across the counter.

"How do you do that?" she asked, reaching for the

sheet, patting him on the shoulder. He finally glanced her way, his thoughts still focused on the electronic chart, and gave her a sideways wink.

"Just situationally aware," he teased, never slowing the pace of his fingers on the keyboard. Amanda was five foot nothing, and he laughed as she fanned herself with the prescription he'd just handed her.

"Dr. Baby, why are all the good-lookin' ones either taken or gay?" she asked absently and then pivoted on her heel, not waiting for an answer. She always shortened his name, teasing him a little about his looks. Both that and her outlandish comment made him chuckle as he pulled his thoughts completely away from the medical record to watch her walk away. This was exactly why he preferred the emergency room to any other department in the hospital—fast-paced with quick-witted, fun people. It said something about all of the ER staff that they purposefully chose this controlled chaos over the day-to-day life of a more structured hospital department.

"Oh, I think I saw Mrs. Burch in the waiting room.

She didn't look happy," Amanda called out, turning back around to face him as she walked down the hall. Her laugh told him he hadn't quite hidden the wince at hearing that information.

"She's here?" Derek questioned, the medical record in front of him now completely forgotten.

"Yep or I'm pretty sure it was her. Want me to go find her?" Kristina offered from across the work area, taking over the conversation where Amanda left off.

"Yeah, if you don't mind."

With a quick bob of her head, she was out of her chair, heading toward the waiting room. Derek closed the chart and looked at his iPad, scanning the patient listings for the Burch name. He stifled a yawn and wondered if she could truly be here at this hour. A glance at his watch showed it was only midnight, which made this entire night seem that much longer. What in the world could she possibly be doing out at this hour?

Derek rubbed a hand over his tired, gritty eyes as he scanned all the patients who were currently waiting to be seen. For the first time that night, the loud background clatter sank in. He glanced out over the waiting room, as well as down the long hall. They'd officially reached standing-room only. Welcome to the summer.

"Burch is in room five," Kristina called out as she walked quickly past him to the patient standing at the desk. Technically Burch should be seen in order of importance. He highly doubted her illness or injury should take precedence over others waiting for a doctor, but he bypassed those ahead of her in queue and went straight toward her room, nodding at a few colleagues as he made his way down the hall.

She deserved to have to wait because he suspected he knew the reason for this visit. Even at eighty-plus years old, Mrs. Burch would most definitely outlive him if nothing more than to prove to him that she could. As he turned the corner, he looked down the hall to see room five's window blinds closed up tight, and he could already sense the drama pouring his way. He hid the smile and forced a frustrated look, causing his brow to crease his forehead. She really had to stop trying to get his attention this way.

"Dr. Babineaux, you have an older female patient in room five who refuses to see anyone but you," a patient care associate said quietly as he passed him, pushing a costume-clad zombie in a wheelchair. No way to know if the blood covering his leg was fake or real. The costume fit voodoo-fest more than spring break, but it was New Orleans after all. Anything went and that always made this time of year more hectic for the entire emergency room. There was never a dull moment since he'd been back, that was for sure.

"Got it," he shot out, all focus back on room number five. Given how tired he was with the sheer volume of patients flowing through their facility, he figured all his co-workers should be frustrated as hell by a visit like this. He'd have to make amends tomorrow night.

He shoved open the door with a little more force than necessary and stepped inside the room. Burch lay there in all her normal sophisticated elegance. She was tall, thin, and fully dressed in a sweater-set and khaki capris, looking very much like an aging model from any nautical magazine you could pick up off the shelf. She slightly turned her head to look his way. Her well-aged face showed a narrowed, furrowed brow, clearly irritated at the small team of nurses that formed around her right arm, trying to draw blood.

"What's wrong with these people? They never get it right the first time. And who's this one? He must be new." She knew them all so the surprise was clear in her voice as she pointed to the man expertly drawing blood from her arm.

"Mrs. Burch, it's always a pleasure," Derek said formally, making his way across the room to stand at the foot of her bed. He brought her record up on his iPad to see a note written in large letters: *She's in a mood tonight*. Derek bypassed that obvious statement and saw nothing in the way of notes indicating why she'd made this trip.

His act of defiance was to ignore everything she had just said to him. Mrs. Burch never gave an inch and her veins were almost non-existent, making things like conversation and blood drawing almost impossible.

"You've had a birthday since I last saw you." Derek

never looked up from the tablet. His smile grew big, but he kept it hidden. He'd missed her birthday yesterday. Damn, he'd be in trouble for that one. So he diverted from that monumental mistake. She'd hate what he was about to say more than him missing the blessed day. "So that makes you eighty-three now, right?"

Tension wafted throughout the room.

"You aren't near correct as usual. I don't know why I keep coming here, you all are always misinformed. Ow!" she gasped, swiping her free hand toward the nurse who untied the rubber tourniquet around her upper arm and withdrew the needle from her vein.

This male nurse was an expert at drawing blood in terrible situations so Derek didn't scold her for trying to move at such a critical time in the process.

"What brings you in to see us on such a busy night? Your vitals look good. And it appears you wouldn't answer any questions for the nurses, so you're being your normal disagreeable self, I see," Derek tossed out. Mrs. Burch ignored him completely. Her frown was now aimed toward the female nurses still in the room. They were probably the first to attempt a needle stick and fail. He knew firsthand what that glare could do to a person. Truth be told, she had scared the shit out of him more than once when that same look landed directly on him as a boy.

Derek looked up, making brief eye contact with each of them, and cocked his head toward the door. He was certain drawing blood was a complete waste of time in this instance. He got a mouthed *'thank you'* before they moved quickly out of the room. The auburn-haired male nurse, Justin, who was working at her arm never lifted his gaze, but Derek knew he was aware of everything going on around him. He was new to the hospital, straight off his third military tour and hadn't lost that military vibe about him—quiet, efficient, always watching, and only spoke when spoken too. There wasn't a time when he wouldn't pitch in to help in any given situation. A total team player, and extremely easy on the eyes.

Mrs. Burch kept her gaze on the male nurse as he quickly and efficiently finished labeling the vials and added them to the cart. He appeared to never notice her stare as he worked. Derek surveyed her arm. She usually left with big ugly bruises already forming on her thin skin, but this time he saw none of the discoloration that typically formed. She didn't acknowledged how quickly the male nurse had done his job when the others couldn't find a vein, but he hadn't missed the sudden interest she'd shown. Her brows lifted as she watched the nurse stroll from the room never looking back at either of them.

"Not even a *'have a goodnight'*?" she stated as the door clicked firmly shut behind him.

"We're alone now. What brings you here so late tonight? You're clearly not sick." Derek anchored a hip on the side of the bed.

"I have hemorrhoids," she offered defiantly. These moments were designed for shock and awe. She just never remembered that he'd seen it all.

"No, you don't, Aunt Vera. Why are you here wasting everyone's time? You could have just called me tomorrow," Derek said, forcing her to scoot over to let him sit fully on the bed.

"You're thirty-five years old and single. I met a young man today I really want you to meet. You didn't answer my telephone calls, so I came here. That silly nurse in triage said you were too busy so I acted sick. Hand me my phone, and I'll show you his picture. The young man took a selfie, or something along those lines. Let me show it to you, I think you might like this one. He's a professional. An accountant. Everyone needs a good accountant in their lives." His aunt had easily pushed herself up on the bed, trying to reach for her purse on the floor. Derek extended his leg and used his foot to scoot the purse away from her grasp.

"You know I'm not interested in your hookups and we're very busy tonight. I don't have time for this now. I love you very much and appreciate the thought, but you have to trust me, I'm fine," Derek replied. His aunt had always been interested in his love life, but about six months ago she had begun to take things to a different level. She stayed on him nonstop to find someone to share his life with. She was always trying to set him up with someone new.

"I promised your mother I would take care of you and you're making me break that promise. Being alone is no kind of life," she countered his automatic refusal with the same argument she always had.

"How did you get here tonight? Tell me you didn't drive."

"I took a cab, if that's any business of yours."

"You promised me that you would take care of yourself. Being out on a night like this is dangerous. There's too much going on, you need to be safe at home. Call me in the morning and we can talk more and schedule lunch for your birthday. I have patients stacked up tonight, I need to go. I'll arrange for you to get home safely, but don't do this again. You aren't as young as you think you are," he explained, helping her from the bed even as she resisted the move.

"You need better nurses. I'm going to be bruised for a week," she pointed out, looking down at her arm. He still didn't see the usual bruising. She'd apparently forgotten what a better experience this blood draw had turned out to be.

Out of all his family, Derek looked the most like her. Green eyes, so similar to his own, sparkled back at him as she looked up at him expectantly. Derek made sure she was steady as she got to her feet. She was almost as tall as his own six-two. He brushed the graying blonde hair out of her face and hoped he'd be able to hang on to his blond as long as she had, but she didn't pay him any attention and moved away, tearing the tape from her arm. Derek didn't try and stop her as she tossed the bandage in the trash. He reached down for her purse and carefully walked her out of the room and down the hall toward the front of the ER entrance. Luckily an ambulance driver he knew was out front, climbing into his truck.

"Hey, TJ," Derek called out after slapping the side of the truck to get the driver's attention before he could shut his door. "Listen, man, I know your shift's over and you're headed back to the station, but can you drop her off at her house? She just lives a few blocks north on Seventh street."

TJ stood on the running board of the ambulance, peering down at them from over the cab of the truck.

“Is she all right?” TJ asked in a deeply Southern voice.

“She’s fine. But I need to make sure she gets home. She can ride in the front and she won’t give you any trouble.” Derek looked over at his aunt, lifting an eyebrow for emphasis as he pulled her along. She’d returned to prattling on about his love life and how he needed someone to go home to, but he ignored her as he helped her inside the passenger seat of the truck.

“I can buckle my own self in,” she exclaimed, knocking his hands away, showing her irritation. He stood back and waited. In the end, she couldn’t navigate the complicated strap and Derek buckled her in.

“Call me in the morning,” he said and tenderly kissed her cheek.

“I didn’t think about that nice, good-looking young man that labeled my blood. What was his name, Derek? What about him? He was very nice to m…” Derek cut her off before she could finish.

“Mom would be proud of your effort, Aunt Vera. I’ve got work to do. Call me in the morning.” Derek looked over to where TJ was settling into the driver's seat. "She lives at five-one-one North Seventh. Can you make sure she gets inside for me?"

TJ laughed as his eyes jumped back and forth between the two of them.

"She's your family, huh?" TJ asked, still chuckling.

"She is," he started but his aunt finished the sentence.

"Not anymore. I'm taking him out of my will. Can you drive me to my attorney's home? He charges enough to be awakened in the middle of the night." Aunt Vera sat back in her seat, crossing her arms over her chest, and stared straight out the front window. That had TJ barking out another laugh and Derek rolling his eyes at her joke. At least he hoped she was joking, he never knew for sure with that woman.

He didn't waste any more time. He leaned forward to give her a quick peck on the cheek and patted her linked fingers on her lap before he closed the door. Derek absently lifted a hand to wave as he jogged the few steps inside. He stopped in his tracks and let out a sigh when he saw the overcrowded waiting room still packed to capacity and no end to the line of patients coming through that door.

~~~

The fast-paced, atmosphere of the night was exactly the kind of challenge Justin enjoyed. Everything around him buzzed with energy and activity, constantly pulling him in many different directions. These kinds of nights reminded him of his time on the front lines. Every deployment had him in the trenches, setting up make-shift triage units and administering care to those who needed it the most.

Those wounds had been dramatically different from the ones coming through Tulane, but he loved the hustle and bustle. It was familiar to him, a sort of security to his unsure soul. Something that kept his mind too busy and away from the thoughts of his self-proclaimed somewhat fucked-up mental state.

His last patient had been a bleeder. Partyers didn't make great patients. This particular incident involved a
~~~

blade-brandishing drunk. Alcohol and knives never mixed, no matter how skilled the trickster thought he was at wielding the blade. They never seemed to learn.

Using his backside to push open the swinging doors, Justin stripped off his scrubs top and tossed the blood-soaked fabric inside the designated bin before grabbing a clean shirt.

"How's it going out there?" Justin jerked, quickly looking over his shoulder, seeing a guy working his shoes off and tossing them in a locker. He'd thought he was alone, and he was usually more cautious about his surroundings.

"Slammed," Justin said, trying to remember the guy's name.

"Welcome to the night shift." He heard the locker shut as he struggled the shirt over his head.

"I like it busy," Justin finally added after a moment's pause. The guy came to a stop in front of him, a backpack slung over his shoulder. Apparently he wanted to talk. "You off?"

"Yeah, I stayed to help out, but I gotta roll. It's

different than the field?"

Justin wasn't sure how to answer the unexpected comment. It didn't sound like a question, so he looked closer at the man to see where this line of conversation might be coming from.

"You doing okay in the transition?"

That had Justin narrowing his brow. As he originally suspected, he should know this guy. He absently looked down at the legs of his scrubs for any leftover blood as he willed himself to remember where he should know him from, but after a minute, he cut his eyes back up and scanned the guy's face.

"You don't remember me, do you? I'm Jack with EAP…the employee assistance program. I met you briefly in orientation. I'm the social worker you're supposed to check in with."

"That's right. Sorry about that, man," Justin apologized, remembering now and doing exactly what he did in orientation when he met the guy. He ducked his head, went for the sink, and scrubbed his hands, ignoring all questions. This guy was all about talking about feelings. No way was Justin into any of that touchy-feely crap and especially not with this guy.

“No problem. Everything going okay?” Justin looked up to see Jack standing behind him. Their eyes met in the mirror. Justin sighed internally and tried not to wince. Jack wasn’t going to be so easily avoided this time.

“Sure,” Justin offered and glanced down as he rinsed the soap off his hands.

“Adjusting well to civilian life?” the guy asked.

“Sure,” Justin offered again, pumping more soap on his hands. He thought the “everything going okay” question covered it all. Why were they still talking?

“You probably wouldn’t tell me otherwise, would you?” the guy asked. Justin waited until he reached for the hand towels to answer. Clearly, Jack wasn’t going anywhere without something from him.

“No, probably not…” Justin answered honestly and tossed the paper towels in the trash. When Jack’s face changed to speculation, he figured the truth wasn’t what he wanted to hear. “I mean, I know you’re there if I need anything.” He felt proud of thinking of that response.

"Right. That's why you remembered me. I'll keep checking in. I'm hearing good things about you. Life's just real different out here. More open. It can get overwhelming."

Justin had no idea what to say to that. The military had prepared him for this when he'd refused another tour. Admittedly, leaving the military hadn't been his first choice. He loved the armed forces, loved the lifestyle and the travel. His life plan had been to make a career out of the military, but his partner didn't like the way they were forced to live and Justin wasn't the kind of guy to buck the system. Besides, he didn't like being away from his partner for those long months either. He never felt right living his life the way he had. Don't ask, Don't tell was still the best approach for some, even if the law had changed—attitude certainly had not. So he made an informed decision and went back to living life as a civilian.

"I'm adapting." All things considered, he thought he was doing pretty okay.

"Cool. I'll be in touch." Jack slapped his upper arm

and pivoted on his feet. He never looked back as Justin watched him leave. The exchange had been kind of unexpected and, the more he thought about it, had come out of nowhere. He'd been there for weeks now—that kind of worried him. He must need to work harder at hiding the stress.

He turned back to the sink, a little confused, and stared at his reflection in the mirror, trying to see what might have given him away. To him, he looked like he always did. He had even trimmed his already short, close-cropped hair today. Maybe he should stop that. Let his hair grow out. That would be another mind-set change, something else to get used to. Besides his super-short hair, he didn't notice anything out of the ordinary. He thought he even fit in to everyday life except he had a sternness to him. Looking in the mirror, he made an effort to relax his facial features. That made him laugh. A forced relaxed face just made him look dumb.

As a pep talk, he reminded himself, he was a master at hiding. He'd hid his entire life and he'd get comfortable soon enough. It wasn't just work, but every part of his life that required a change in mind-set. He'd get used to things eventually, he had to. There was more than just him to consider. His partner had given up so much to be with him. Surely he'd give him a little more time to adapt to the private sector.

Besides, he did have some solids going for him. Justin was emotionally comfortable with his sexual orientation, regardless of the tension building between him and his partner. His recent reservations had nothing to do with his sex life and everything to do with the feelings of inadequacy he'd also carried around for most of his life. Hopefully time would heal some of that, and if not, then he'd deal with that when the time came. He'd learned a long time ago not to bring on worries before he needed to.

Shoving open the locker room door, he squared his broad shoulders and went back to the rat race, leaving those troubled thoughts behind.

CHAPTER 2

Hours passed before the emergency room slowed to a manageable pace. Derek dropped down in an abandoned chair in the back of the nurses' station and dug his thumb and forefinger into his eyes. The non-stop frantic tempo he'd walked into on this shift had started to abate. He stifled a yawn as he rolled his shoulders and looked up at the big wall clock. It was four fifteen in the morning. Way past the time things should have slowed down for the hospital on a Wednesday night.

"Dr. Baby," came a quiet whisper. Derek looked around at the empty station and then did a full circle in the chair, still not seeing anyone. He rose and walked in the general direction of the voice. He slowly peeked around the corner and found Amanda, Kristina, and Kylie, three of the nightshift nurses, standing together, all staring intently at something.

"Did you call me?" he asked.

"Shhhh," they said in unison, waving their hands, but never looking back at him.

"He's hot," Amanda cooed softly.

"Yeah, he is," Kristina affirmed the spoken thought.

"Too bad he's taken," Kylie offered and Derek wondered if he should wipe the metaphorical drool from her chin.

"Are you sure?" Kristina asked.

"Yeah, or at least that's what he told Ally." The collective sigh turned to disappointment. Derek smiled at the back of their heads. These three women were top notch, well-educated, seasoned nurses who were acting like teenage girls watching their crush on television.

"Who are you watching?" Derek whispered and peered around them. His eyes connected with the handsome nurse's form as he used his brute strength to lift an incoming patient from a wheelchair to a gurney.

Okay, he got it now. Damn, that was hot.

"The new hire, Justin Delacroix. Check out those biceps," Kylie whispered.

"Screw the biceps, did you see how the fabric stretched across his back. I bet there isn't an ounce of fat on the guy," Kristina offered just as quietly.

"And he told Ally he was dating someone?" Derek asked, now fully invested in admiring the view. The broad shoulders and thin waist were hot in and of themselves, but when he bent over to secure the gates, he caught a glimpse of the deeply tanned skin peeking from under the scrubs.

"No, he lives with someone. It's serious." Again the disappointment was deep in Amanda's voice.

"I like his hair color," Kristina whispered.

"I like his body. All that tall, muscular, tanned flesh…" Kylie wiped her chin this time.

"Most auburn-haired people don't get that tan," Amanda added.

"Right. And he doesn't have freckles. Does that make him Brazilian?" Kristina asked.

"It makes him hot as hell," Amanda declared.

Derek watched as Ally, the charge nurse, approached the new hire. "I'll take the patient from here. But can I get you to run something down to the lab for me? I can't get a lab-tech down here and it's important," he overheard the charge nurse ask. The nurses then scattered, knocking into themselves in order to avoid being caught staring.

"Sure, what am I taking?" Derek loved the deep, smooth tone of his voice. The three female nurses all pretended to be busy before Justin turned back their way. At that point Derek was the only one standing there, not doing anything, hands tucked into his lab coat and a smile stretched across his face, which had turned to laughter at the terrible acting skills he'd just witnessed from the nurses. Justin glanced his way but was clearly confused by his reaction. The male nurse's brow narrowed and he openly stared at Derek. Justin's hard-edged look turned him on, and he stood there, gawking, as the fatigue from earlier faded and his dick awakened inside his briefs.

With all those good looks staring back at him and that big, muscular frame within easy reach, he tended to agree with the nurses' astute observations. He figured he could find it in himself to go a round or two with the male nurse.

"Amanda has it. I'll call the lab to tell them to expect you. It's a rush," he heard Ally reply. Derek turned, anchoring his shoulder against the wall. From his vantage point, he could see the entire inner workings of the nurses' station. Amanda now sat at a terminal, typing away. The way her hands flew over the keyboard, Derek wasn't certain she was even creating words. Justin took a few tentative steps toward the nurses' station.

"Amanda?" the male nurse asked quietly, clearly trying to remember who was who.

"Amanda's at the computer," Derek said, helping him out.

Justin nodded and approached the desk. "Do you have the lab work?" That rich baritone voice had that half erection turning full and hard. Since all eyes were on Justin, Derek easily reached down to adjust himself, making sure he was completely hidden as he watched Amanda's flushed face lift to Justin. All she did was point to the box on the desk. The new nurse looked at everyone again, still completely confused at what he'd missed, but picked up the box and didn't say another word as he headed down the hall toward the double doors.

"Damn, those eyes were made for sin. They look golden!" Kristina whispered when the coast was clear. She dramatically fanned herself with the file folder. She craned her neck, trying to catch a final glimpse as Justin walked away.

"No kidding! He can have me any day," Amanda said, theatrically flailing her arms as she slumped in the seat. She threw her head back against the head rest and sighed loudly.

"We're in a hospital, you know," Derek said dryly, the lab coat covering the evidence of his attraction.

"Whatever, Dr. Babineaux. You know you want him, but I get him first," Kylie declared and he just grinned.

"I'm sure I should be saying something about

appropriate behavior and all that nonsense. I've got work to do. Call me if you need me, but only if you need me. I'll be in the office, getting caught up." The cackle he got from the three of them made it clear they weren't buying his lackadaisical response. Whatever. He had a hot male nurse to go scope out.

CHAPTER 3

Justin handed over the lab work and left without asking directions back, even though he'd gotten lost three times on the way there. It had taken him some time to remember the way. The lab was across the hospital complex and there were too many closed halls and darkened walkways to easily navigate the route, but he was a smart guy. He didn't need to ask for directions. He'd figure his way back and forth soon enough.

The error of that decision landed squarely on his shoulders with the fourth wrong turn and retracing he had to do. Navigating all the turns in daylight hours proved difficult for a new hire because the campus was massive, bigger than anyplace he'd ever worked before, but at night, with the quiet, lowered lighting, and lack of constant foot traffic, it was almost impossible. The years of slow expansion led to a hodgepodge of hallways in some areas—he'd think he was headed in the right direction and wind up in a ghost town of rooms and empty stations.

"Hey!" A familiar voice broke the silence of the empty corridor. Startled, he spun around.

"It's a big place. I get turned around when everything's so quiet like this." Justin made a quick excuse as he came to a stop right in front of Dr. Babineaux.

"The ER's back there," Dr. Babineaux offered, staring at Justin with that signature sexy crooked grin spreading across his face. He tossed a thumb over his shoulder to indicate the direction, but never broke eye contact. "Follow me."

It took a moment before Derek finally swiveled on his heels, and Justin hid a smile, waiting a second before he followed. After several feet of walking a step or two behind the man, Derek finally said, "You're adapting well. I've had many patient compliments about you tonight."

"I don't know about that. It's pretty different out here," Justin spoke quietly, looking down at his feet with each step he took.

"You're really doing great. But you're quiet and always intense," Derek said, glancing over his shoulder as he slowed to let Justin catch up.

They kept a professional distance apart as they walked, something Justin always insisted upon since the first minute he'd started working at Tulane. Derek slowed his pace a bit more as he turned, leading them down another darkened hall.

"You've never really seen me in full battlefield trauma mode before," Justin finally answered when it appeared Derek was waiting for his response. The concerned look morphed to one of fun in a matter of a few seconds.

"You look sexy in those scrubs," Derek murmured. The doctor was flirting with him. Those moments seemed to be coming with more regularity. Since Justin was more of an actions-speak-louder-than-words kind of guy, he ignored the comment completely, but god, he wanted to kiss that smirk right off the handsome doctor's face. If he said something, Derek would only be encouraged to continue that line of thought, and they wouldn't ever make it back, so he kept quiet and looked down the hall. He tried to judge their distance from where they were compared to the actual emergency room, but he couldn't. He'd followed Derek on yet another turn he hadn't expected and they were now headed down an abandoned corridor. He must have been even farther off course than he'd thought. He couldn't even locate any security cameras down this particular seemingly unused hallway.

Derek abruptly bumped his shoulder. He glanced over at the doctor, wondering how they'd ended up walking so closely together. The sexy, come-hither grin was solidly there. That smile always messed with his insides, causing the faint tingles of desire to stir and shoot straight to his dick. So not a good thing, especially at work. Thank god they were completely alone.

Justin forced himself to look away from a teasing Derek, but his heart still picked up another beat and his cheeks heated. He wasn't a flirt, never had been, and certainly not while working. He had watched and learned there were lots of inappropriate lines crossed between the staff at the hospital, but all in a playful, innocent, fun kind of way.

The problem with teasing innocent thoughts? He couldn't remember a time that those ever applied to Derek. He was a fun-loving guy. Up for anything at any time and that made him incredibly dangerous to play with.

Besides, Derek Babineaux was about the hottest thing he'd ever seen. The man was tall, about his own height, broad and lean, with a face sculpted like that of a Greek god. His olive complexion and jade green eyes regularly stole his breath and his heart. Justin swore those eyes had the ability to bore right through his soul every time Derek looked his way. The doctor's blond hair always had a bit of a wave, especially after a long hard night in the emergency room. He loved that sexy disheveled look—loved it more than he was willing to admit. And the handsome doctor spent time in the gym, no question there, that muscled body gave him a hard-on every time he stole a glance Derek's direction.

He quickly weighed his options, deciding in the name of innocent fun, he needed to give as good as he got. Surely he could play along on this level in an effort to try and fit in a little better around there.

"I'm starting to think you might have a crush on me, Dr. Baby." His own crooked smile spread, hoping he was getting past the too quiet remark from earlier. He didn't want Derek to see him that way.

"Then quit dodging me and let's play doctor," Derek growled. Justin could feel Derek's heated gaze on him, but refused to look his way.

"I don't mix business with pleasure," Justin playfully fired right back, like he had every night they'd worked together. Besides, Derek had to know he was such a liar. It took everything in him not to jump the smug doctor right there in the hallway and show him exactly how well he played with others.

"I'm not buying it. Besides, if you don't want to play with me, then why do I always catch you eye-fucking me?" Derek cockily countered. The doctor grabbed his forearm, stopping Justin in his tracks. Derek turned toward him and their eyes locked in an instant. Justin wondered if Derek could hear his heart pounding against his chest as he held his challenging gaze.

This was new to the game.

"Eye-fucking you? Seriously?" Justin laughed, making it a point to let his eyes roam slowly over Derek's body. After the briefest of pauses at seeing the evidence of Derek's arousal, he lifted his eyes. "I never said I didn't want to play with you, I just said I don't mix business with pleasure."

"And neither do I." Derek caught him off guard. He wrapped an arm around his waist and tugged him inside a closet that Justin hadn't even noticed was there.

Seconds later, the lock on the door clicked, and he was shoved against the tile wall before he had time to protest. There was just enough light in the small space for Justin to swear he saw a wicked glint flash in Derek's eyes as he lifted a hand, holding him easily in place. His breath deepened. He refused to consider the consequences. No way was he going to move one single muscle. His heart slammed in his chest and his desire kicked up steam.

Derek's lip curled as he leaned in closer, clearly reading him like a book. Yeah, there was definitely a challenge reflected in those green eyes. Nothing but silence filled the room as they stared at one another in those first few provocative seconds.

"I want you so fucking bad I hurt." Derek was on him. So close he could smell the fresh clean scent of his expensive cologne and feel the heat of the other man's arousal rubbing along his. Damn, Dr. Derek Babineaux was as turned on as he was.

"Is it safe here?" Justin asked, not moving, but needing to touch the hot doctor so badly.

"Hell if I know. I've never done this before," Derek whispered. Words like that were always Justin's undoing. Warm, soft lips pressed against his. The weight of Derek's firm body pinned him against the wall. He heard himself whimper when Derek's tongue pushed between his lips and the kiss deepened, becoming a frenzy of tongues and teeth, exploring and probing, tasting and teasing. Justin melted into his arms. His knees were now as weak as his resolve. He couldn't think, not that he needed to, his instincts had already taken over as he grabbed Derek's ass and pulled the doctor closer against him. Derek swiveled his hips, grinding them hard into his already aching cock.

"You make me so hard!" Derek hissed as he broke from the kiss to trail his nose along Justin's neck. He rolled his hips forward, grinding his rigid cock into Derek's. "Oh yeah, I want you…bad."

Derek's hands were all over him, kneading and caressing before slipping under the hem of his scrubs. Warm palms slid up his ribs and skated across his tightening nipples. God, he loved that move. His nipples hardened to small nubs under the sensual assault. Why he'd waited so long to give in to these suggestions was beyond him. They'd danced around each other since the first day he'd started work.

"Wanted you from day one…" Justin whispered. Derek slid a hand between them, the action causing the slightest brush across his already aching cock as the man worked to pull something from his pocket. The sensation set him on fire. Just the merest touch from Derek and he was lost. Two small packets were pushed into his hand as the doctor's lab coat fell away. Derek was back at his neck, running his lips over his throat, sending chills coursing through his body. Recognition made his dick twitch when Justin realized what he held in his hand. Did Derek carry protection around in his pocket all the time? Justin's eyes dropped to the foil packages in his palm. Lifting a brow, he glanced back up at Derek and placed the packages on the shelf beside him. "That sure of yourself, huh?"

That sly grin slid across Derek's lips, curling at the tips, lighting up his eyes. "I'm that sure, are you?"

Derek's words hit a chord inside him. Was he sure? Even though he wasn't in the military any longer, he knew what would happen if they were caught. He also knew he'd have to discourage these encounters in the future, while he was on hospital time, but he couldn't find it in him to care at the moment.

Enshrouded behind the thin cotton material of his scrubs, his dick ached to be touched and it was the only thought looping through his mind. They didn't have much time, surely they would be missed. This would be a quickie, but that thought faded as soon as Derek grabbed his ass. The doctor clearly left nothing to chance and forced his hips up higher, guiding his cock against the hardness already pressed into him.

Justin captured Derek's lips with his. He poured all he had into that kiss, savoring the sweetness of Derek's mouth working against his. Damn, the doctor could kiss. Derek's tongue slid against his and the kiss deepened. The craving to sample the rest of the tempting doctor grew too hard to resist. He untied Derek's scrubs and worked his hand in between their heated bodies, circling the doctor's thick shaft with his fingers.

"Ahh, yeah…feels so good," Derek hissed, breaking from the kiss, and started rocking into his fist.

Justin wouldn't let him go. He took Derek's mouth

with his, sucking his tongue in deep, like he wanted to do to his dick. Derek's kiss turned aggressive as they ate at each other's mouths. Warm breath and the sweet taste of Derek's lips mingled with his, clouded his judgment, but screw it, he wanted this. The sound of heavy breathing filled the dimly lit room. He was flying, soaring with amatory emotion. That they might be caught added a level of intensity that spurred on the need coursing in him. He opened wider, Derek's tongue pushed and swirled around his, both men fighting for dominance. The scent of their arousal hung in the air as he massaged Derek's cock with sure, strong strokes.

Justin dropped to his knees, pulling Derek's scrubs and briefs down his thighs before he buried his face in Derek's groin.

"I've been wanting this so bad," Derek growled, threading his hands in Justin's short hair. He ran his fingers along Derek's dick before gripping all that hardness in his fist and placing a kiss to the tip. He slid his tongue in the small slit and lapped at the crown before running his lips up the thick vein. Justin glanced up. He needed to see Derek's face. Their eyes met, and he held Derek's gaze as he opened his mouth and swallowed him down to the root.

Hollowing his cheeks, he sucked harder. His eyes rolled to the back of his head, and he was in heaven. He'd dreamed about sucking this cock since the first night he'd laid eyes on Derek and that hadn't changed one single time since. He savored the sweet essence of Derek's pre-come coating his tongue. Frantic fingers played in his hair as he ran his tongue along that sensitive ridge.

He wanted to please Derek, make him crazy with desire.

"Oh shit…I've been meaning to properly welcome you to the staff since you started here," Derek panted, holding on to Justin's short hair and working his hips to the rhythm Justin created.

The odd remark caught Justin off guard, so he looked up. Derek's head was bowed toward him, and his eyes were closed. Pleasure painted across that beautiful face. Justin reached up and cupped Derek's balls, fondling the tender sac while working the velvety length with his mouth, sucking him deep before pulling away.

"I'm very impressed with the welcome so far, Dr. Baby." Justin played with Derek's sac, enjoying the feel and weight in his palm. He smiled at the little humming noises Derek made when he began exploring the area between the doctor's balls and his ass.

As he continued the gentle massage, he sucked his finger into his mouth. Seconds later, he smoothed his hand around the globes of Derek's ass, before sliding the moist digit into Derek's crevice. The hands in his hair tightened as he pressed snugly against Derek's rim. He circled and teased the tight ring of muscle with his thumb, then pressed his wet finger slowly into Derek's heat, stretching him open. Justin added a second and third finger, working the doctor with his digits as he went back to devouring his cock.

At the moment Justin was so fucking turned on that he wouldn't have cared who walked in on them. He wasn't going to let up till they made memories of their own in the hospital supply room.

"Stop, I don't wanna come yet," Derek hissed loudly. The fingers in his hair firmly holding him back. "I want you in me when I come."

Justin withdrew his fingers, kissing his way up Derek's body as he stood. The way Derek looked at him made Justin weak with need. He was already right there with him, ready to be buried balls deep in that sweet tight ass.

Derek licked his bottom lip, drawing Justin's attention to the doctor's kiss-swollen lips. He couldn't resist the temptation and took Derek's mouth in a heated kiss. His tongue curled and swirled around Derek's, dipping deep, and Derek returned the kiss, moaning into his mouth. Justin couldn't get enough of this man. Couldn't get enough of his kiss, his taste, his body. Derek suddenly pushed Justin's scrubs and underwear down his thighs. The cool air hit his heated skin, sending a shiver up his spine. He gasped as a warm palm wrapped around his aching cock and began stroking him with long, lazy pulls.

Damn, Derek's hand felt amazing on him. No way

was he going to last under this assault. Justin broke from the kiss, trying to hang on to his sanity as he grabbed the small packages off the shelf and handed the condom to Derek.

The doctor opened and rolled the condom on him with skilled hands. His skill showed this was certainly something he'd done a time or two before. And fuck if it wasn't one of the sexiest things he'd ever witnessed. Justin lifted the lube to his lips and tore open the foil packet before drizzling a good amount on to his fingers and cock. He tossed the package into an empty Styrofoam cup sitting on a shelf.

"How much time do we have?" Justin panted.

"We have time. I'm on a break and you're lost." Derek hadn't taken his eyes off him. Damn, that man oozed sex and the heated look in his green eyes shot straight to Justin's dick in pulses of white-hot need.

Justin leaned in and captured Derek's mouth in another hot and heavy kiss before spinning him around, pushing his scrubs even lower, and forcing his chest against the wall. Derek's palms slid up the tile and he stuck his bare ass out. *Oh, hell!* The challenge was back. Justin kicked at Derek's legs, urging him to spread them wider, which he did. Their bodies fit perfectly together, just like he knew they would. Justin rolled his hips and groaned loudly when his cock slipped along the crevice of Derek's ass.

"I want you in me, now." Derek pressed his ass back and writhed against him. Justin almost lost it in that moment, and he wasn't even inside the man yet. He worked his hands over the roundness of Derek's firm backside, taking a second to admire, and kneaded the warm flesh with his palms. Smooth, olive-toned skin with a light dusting of fine blond hairs, the man's ass was pure perfection.

He pulled Derek's left cheek to the side, exposing him, and pressed two slick fingers into his tight passage, making sure he was good and open for him. Derek groaned as Justin pumped his fingers in and out of his tight channel. Twisting his wrist, he found that spongy spot that made Derek squirm.

"Fuck me, please," Derek begged, pushing back hard

on Justin's probing digits.

Withdrawing his fingers, he gripped his own cock, running it up and down the already slick crevice of Derek's ass. He circled and teased the opening before slipping the tip of his cock through the tight ring of muscle.

"Fuck, babe," Justin moaned as he slid balls deep into Derek's hot ass. Justin froze as the tight heat gripped him. Unexpected need coursed through his veins, making him afraid to move for fear he'd blow his load. As his heart drummed in his chest, he could hear Derek panting and feel the muscles in his thighs quivering under the strain of this position.

"You feel so good," he breathed into Derek's thick hair. His hands went to Derek's hips to help steady himself. He found it hard to stand when his knees were so weak. Derek writhed back against him and rolled his hips, making Justin moan even louder. This time with unintelligible words, even to his own ears. After a few short thrusts, they settled into a steady rhythm of fucking. Justin smoothed his hand around Derek's firm stomach and kept sliding down until he palmed his dick, giving him a few tugs and running his thumb across the leaking slit before stroking him with purpose. With every thrust of his hips, his orgasm built, the heat of Derek's tight passage coaxing his release.

With one arm wrapped around the doctor, he pressed his chest against Derek's muscular back, kissing the nape of his neck and nibbling at his skin as he drove himself deeper into his lover. He ran his fingers through Derek's thick hair, tugging his head to the side, and took his mouth with a sizzling kiss.

His hips pistoned wildly, driving in and out of Derek's body. The familiar heat started in his spine, coiling around his belly, and landed inside his balls. He struggled to fight off his release.

"Come for me." Justin was so close he barely managed the words.

"Augh…fuck…yes," Derek panted. It seemed all the encouragement he needed. Derek's sweet ass contracted around him, quickly driving Justin up and over the edge.

"Yeah, baby…just like that," Justin barked and thrust

deeper. The sound of flesh slapping flesh filled the small room. Derek's breath hitched and hot come spilled over Justin's fingers. "So fucking good, Derek."

The rush of Derek's release took his breath, and his orgasm crashed over him in waves of sheer pleasure. His mind went numb as his dick jerked and twitched, filling the condom deep in Derek's hot ass. Seconds later, he collapsed against Derek's back, completely spent. Heavy pants filled the room. Justin stayed just like that until his body settled back to normal. He could feel his heart still hammering against his chest and wondered if Derek felt it too, because he could feel Derek's.

"*Fuck!* That was amazing." Justin placed a soft kiss against Derek's shoulder before he gripped the end of the condom and carefully pulled out of his lover. He took another step back as he tied off the condom and dropped it in the empty coffee cup he would have to dispose of later. Derek pressed the length of his firm body back against him, and he wasn't in any hurry to let the man go. He loved the feel of Derek's body against his.

He hid the small smile, burying his nose in Derek's

hair, breathing him in. The doctor was a cuddler, nothing wrong with that. Hell, he hadn't wanted to move either. The moment felt so right and their bodies fit perfectly together. He thought he could hold Derek just like this all night long.

Justin ran his nose up the side of Derek's neck and again inhaled the citrus spice of his lover's cologne mingled with the smell of sex filling the room. The combination had his dick plumping again. If Derek knew what was good for him, he'd break contact. Otherwise they might not ever leave this closet. Seconds later, as if he knew Justin's thoughts, Derek turned in his arms.

"Yes, that was fucking amazing." Derek grinned and pressed a kiss to his lips, wrapping Justin tighter in his arms. Derek's hips rolled forward and his half hard cock ground into his. Damn if Justin wasn't ready for more.

"You're a tease, not to mention probably a really bad influence on me." Justin gave Derek a quick peck before regretfully stepping out of the warm embrace to find something to clean his hand. He pulled his briefs and scrubs up. Their little tryst had to end before either of them were missed.

"I plan on doing a lot of influencing where you're concerned, Mr. Delacroix." Derek chuckled and waggled his eyebrows at him as he cleaned himself up and set his clothes right. Justin loved how they easily connected with one another. He wished they could be open like this in public. Let the world know they were a committed couple, but he knew it was his decisions that held them back.

Justin shook his head, pushing those thoughts away, and forced a grin. "See that's exactly what I'm talking about. You're a bad influence. Now let's go, Romeo. Make sure it's safe to leave."

CHAPTER 4

Derek ever so slightly cracked the door open, carefully peeking out. The hall was still as dark as ever, and from this angle, he could tell no one was coming, but he listened for a second more before he forced the door wider to look down the other end. He'd thought this closed wing would be a good hiding place. He'd heard others talking about trysts they'd shared down this hall. Thankfully the coast was clear. He knew he was flushed. He'd taken too long in the closet, but Justin had a way of making him take chances. This man absorbed all of Derek's coherent thoughts, making him act on sheer impulse and need. Time stood still when he was with Justin.

On that thought, he reached for his phone to make sure he hadn't missed anything. He could completely lose himself in Justin and miss his on-call messages.

"We're good," Derek said, stepping out of the closet. Justin followed immediately behind him. Derek watched with a little frustration as the deer-in-the-headlights look crossed Justin's face. He quickly glanced left, then right as he scanned either side of the hall. He knew from too many years of personal experience, he needed to step away and give Justin room to recover, but that just wasn't who he was as a man.

Derek had known the minute he opened that door, exactly when Justin had taken that mental step back and let the wall drop back in place. Now Justin kept several feet away from him and that caused a small shard of pain to slice his heart. While Derek stared at the distance between them, a sad realization shrouded him—his love and devotion to this man might not ever be enough to make him comfortable, no matter how hard he tried.

Apparently, you could take the man out of the military, but not the military out of the man. His heart broke a little more with that recurring thought. "No one knows. I promise."

"Cameras have to be stationed somewhere in this hall, even though you can't see them." Justin's voice was almost a whisper.

"This part of the building's closed. They don't monitor here," Derek said, taking another step backward, giving Justin more room. He left off the part *that he was guessing*, he really didn't know for sure.

Justin carried the small cup that held tangible proof of the passion they had just shared, the only thing left connecting them to the moment of lovemaking they had just experienced.

Derek resisted all urges to touch Justin as he turned and started walking down the long corridor. Justin tossed away the cup at the first available trashcan they passed. He gave an inward sigh when he heard Justin's footsteps following a step or two behind. He'd wanted their moment together, even pushed for this since Justin first began at Tulane. His friends, who were couples, had lovingly shared stolen moments. He'd heard those stories for years, and they meant something special to each person who'd shared them. He'd just wanted that same feeling with his significant other.

Truthfully, tonight he may have grown a little possessive while listening to the nurses talk about Justin. Maybe that was why he set this up, but now he was second-guessing his decision. He wanted a relationship where he didn't have to hide. One with open glances and quick make-out sessions even in public places, regardless of the professionalism of their jobs. He watched those happen to the couples he'd worked with too. Dammit, stolen moments meant something to the relationship.

"Shit, it's already four forty-five. My shift's supposed to end at six. I'm gonna be late. I've gotta get some things done before I can leave." Derek glanced back up, hid his wayward thoughts, and let the naughty grin he knew Justin liked spread across his face. Justin surrendered to it and briefly gave him that gentle after-sex look he loved the most, the one that made him melt.

"Whoever gets out of here first needs to stop and pick

up some dog food for Gunner and Gracie before we go home. I didn't get to it yesterday. If you do that, I'll grab us some beignets and a couple of decaf café au laits. We might be able to get a couple hours sleep before you head out to your parents' anniversary party tonight," Derek said.

"Sure," Justin murmured absently and their moment was gone. They had reached the emergency room hallway. Justin pushed through the double doors, never looking back, leaving Derek standing there watching him walk away as the doors swung shut.

~~~

Justin stopped in the middle of the hall and turned back to the electronic doors. Was that pain he'd just seen in Derek's eyes? He immediately began to chastise himself. Of course that was pain. It was the same look he'd seen more often than not in Derek's eyes over the last few months. He hadn't understood why.

He resisted the urge to go back and confront that
~~~

look. They'd just had incredible sex where he got to top. He knew Derek had done that on purpose because he loved to be buried balls deep inside that perfect ass. The truth, and what no one knew, was that was the only time in his life he felt whole. Making love to Derek wiped his world clean. Those minutes gave him hope that they were truly a perfect match. Making love to Derek put them on a level playing field. He got as good as he gave.

Realizing he was taking the steps back to Derek, he forced himself to stop. They didn't do this, or better yet, he didn't do this. He wasn't going to pry. When Derek wanted him to know what was going on, he would tell him. Until then, he'd sit back and wait, worrying the whole time.

Justin turned and forced himself down the hall. He'd been gone far too long for the lost excuse to be plausible. He had work to do; he had a job to perform. One that he was damn lucky to have. Derek was responsible for this job. Hell, he was responsible for everything good Justin had in the world. The needling prickles of inadequacy came flooding back. What if that look meant Derek was having second thoughts and just didn't want to tell him?

Then Justin would go with his dignity intact. He schooled his facial features to hide his own pain.

"Stop overthinking everything," he berated himself in the quiet, deserted hall. They had too many years under their belt, too much time to get past the very big difference between them. Yet Derek's aunt had freaked him out tonight. He knew Derek came from money. Besides the way he carried himself, his education spoke for itself. The Babineaux's were a long-established family and very well known in this area.

He'd also never hid that he grew up on the wrong side of town. His parents' two-bedroom home had been filled with four boys. He was the only one of the bunch that hadn't wound up in prison a time or two.

But Derek's aunt reeked of old money and threw it around like a heavy weight. He knew her kind well. They were like the ones that always brought boxes of food to his parents' house during the holidays when he was a boy. It didn't matter that his parents were good people, or that they tried as hard as they could to make a living.

Even at a young age, he could see the judgment in the socialites' eyes as they looked around the meager home and over all their family's circumstance.

"Let it go, Delacroix. Everything changes. Let it go," he whispered to himself. He pushed the insecurity away and concentrated on the sex he'd just had with the man he loved. That memory had his scowl fading. He'd gotten a taste of Derek's ass in the closet and no one knew. That didn't mean he could do that regularly, but damn, this job just got better and better. Maybe he needed to carry his own supply of condoms and lube for the future. He wondered how surprised Derek would be if he pulled those out of his wallet and dropped them in his hand.

Oh yeah, totally surprised. He needed to make sure that happened, soon.

CHAPTER 5

Biting at his fingernail, Derek kicked back in his oversized office chair and waited. He had about a million different administrative tasks he could be performing, but this particular shift had worn him out on more than one level. He decided well over an hour ago that he'd catch up on those paperwork details later. But for now, he just sat there, waiting. Justin had texted him a while ago, letting him know he was running further behind than he'd thought and Derek found he didn't want to leave the hospital without him, even though he'd arranged to see his aunt after he got off work.

Did not wanting to leave without Justin make him insecure? No, of course not. He was just a man in love, he reasoned to himself.

Well, maybe it did make him a little insecure, but it was the same emotional insecurity he'd dealt with for the last five or so years.

Maybe he still hadn't gotten completely used to Justin being home all the time. It seemed they had always just settled back into life when Justin got orders to go again. Or perhaps this round of insecurity had to do with the weeks long anticipated closet sex they'd shared tonight. When Justin landed this job, Derek had begun plotting the best possible ways to get him alone. It took time and diligence, but the effort paid off. Finally.

What he hadn't considered was how much that one sexual act would mean to him. They were fluid at home. They shared lots of those moments behind the closed doors of their house, but never, ever in public—most definitely not in such a risky environment.

How would Justin have acted if they were caught? Would he have distanced himself even further?

Derek had been wrong to assume everything would easily fall into place once Justin left the military. They were months out and completely relocated. Their home set up, yet they were no closer to being out as a couple than before. At least before, Derek had the hope inside his heart that one day they'd have a normal relationship, but now, as each day passed, those thoughts began to fade.

Derek closed his eyes and scolded himself. Self-doubt was the least attractive trait to him. Why would he allow himself to wallow now? Since the beginning, Derek had known Justin was for him. They'd met five years ago. Justin was about to be reassigned and relocated. He spent his leave time back in his hometown, partying in New Orleans.

Derek had been downtown that night at a bachelor party hosted by a friend. Tristan Wilder had been a onetime-patient-turned-friend who had planned a destination bachelor party for the COO of Wilder Inc., Landry Prescott. Even though the eye-candy in the bar that evening had been tempting, Derek couldn't help but be drawn to the auburn-haired man he spotted out on the street. Derek watched through the window as Justin eyed some men who were walking by. The longing in the gaze told him what he needed to know—Justin was gay—and Derek made a beeline straight for the guy.

That shy, quiet, unsure attitude, along with those devilish good looks and hot as hell body endeared Justin to him from almost the first handshake. They enjoyed that night together. It hadn't taken too much persuasion to get Justin back to his place and Derek had pretty much glued himself to him since that moment. Within a few months, he even quit his job, packed up, and moved cross country to set up house with the guy. How risky had that been? He'd given up everything for Justin and no one in their lives even knew.

During the long months of deployment, Derek had stayed faithful. As far as he knew Justin had too. Things were always perfect when Justin came home. They did everything together, from cooking to laundry, even the yard work. During their downtime, they would cuddle on the couch, play video games, watch movies, or even read to each other, and their sex life was beyond amazing. Justin was an attentive lover, always knowing exactly what he needed and making sure he was taken care of. He'd wanted that kind of relationship with this man from the first moment they met.

When the United States legislators repealed Don't ask, Don't tell, he had rejoiced, but it seemed just a theory to Justin. His lover still wouldn't come out to his team or anyone else for that matter. Derek hid the disappointment of keeping the relationship secreted, only because they fit well together and he was a man truly and deeply in love. Justin was his perfect match. If soul mates existed, he'd met his—the one man who fit so well with him that nothing else on the planet seemed to matter.

The decision not to reenlist had been a complicated one. Derek treaded carefully around the issue. Once Justin decided against reenlistment, the decision to move back to New Orleans, hometown to both, had been easy. When he returned a few months before Justin, he easily got his old job back at Tulane, but everyone he went to medical school with was climbing up the corporate ladder. Something he had envisioned for himself all those years ago before he ever met Justin.

A knock on the door took him from his musings. He sat up in the chair and scrubbed a hand over his face. “Yes,” he finally called out and the door opened.

“I’m out of here. I’m bringing my mom’s peanut butter fudge tomorrow night? She’s making it for you. You working?” Amanda asked.

“Yeah, I think so,” Derek said, sitting up further in his seat, shuffling the paperwork on his desk to find the schedule he knew was around there, somewhere.

“What’s wrong?” she asked and stepped all the way inside the office, closing the door behind her. They’d been friends for years. Stayed in touch when he’d moved away, yet he’d never breathed Justin’s name out loud to her.

“Nothing really,” Derek said, concealing the turmoil coursing through him. If he were going to talk to anyone, it would be Amanda, but the thing about hiding made him bury all this inside him, away from everyone.

“Does it have to do with your guy?”

Derek stared at her for several long moments. This

ate at him. The resentment apparently had begun to take on a life of its own. If he didn't get this off his chest, he'd dump this on Justin, and he didn't want that to happen with everything he was already dealing with.

"We're still keeping our relationship hidden." Derek covered his face as he let the words spill out.

"Why?" Amanda asked, taking a seat in front of his desk.

"I don't know. I'd shout it off the roof tops if he'd let me. I guess I just thought things would be different for us after he got out of the military. " Derek leaned back, the fingernail was back in his mouth, and he bit at the corner.

"Do you tell him that?" Amanda offered.

"Somewhat, but I don't want to push him. I want him to make this decision." Derek felt the familiar longing rush across his heart. He guessed that was his bottom line. He wanted Justin to want them bad enough to make the next move.

"Push him, Derek. You have to do something. You look tense, like you're walking on eggshells most of the time. It's not fair you have to hide the relationship like you do. This is so unlike the Derek Babineaux I know."

He contemplated those words. She was right on many levels. It wasn't in his nature to just sit and wait. He had to admit the waiting was taking its toll and it was hard keeping quiet, especially with Justin now working with him every day. But love made you do crazy things, didn't it?

He had thought once Justin was out of the military and settled in his new job, things would immediately be different. That was dumb. Justin needed time to adjust. He was allowing himself to get beat down for no reason. He needed to quit trying to read things into the relationship where Justin was concerned. The vibration from his cell phone drew his attention away from his thoughts. He palmed it, checked the number, and saw it was Justin.

"This is him now," Derek said, lifting the phone off his desk, swiping his finger across the screen to open the message.

"Bye. See you with the fudge tomorrow," she said,

leaving as quickly as she came.

~~~

Justin changed into his street clothes before grabbing a bottle of orange juice from the staff lounge. He sent a short text to Derek, letting him know he was heading out. He'd gotten his work done quickly, not having to stay on too much longer after the shift change. Derek had been on duty longer than anyone this shift, so he figured he was long gone by now.

Justin planned to stop by their favorite bakery on his way home to get Derek his beloved beignets, even though he had said he would do it. He should have just volunteered to grab both the dog food and powdered treats when they talked earlier. He'd have to remember to help do those little things in the future. Derek had earned a little tender love from the years of keeping up their home in his absence. His lover had always made his time home from deployments special. That thought caused Justin to lower his head and smile to himself. The
~~~

private sector did have its own distinct advantages—hot closet sex with the man you love helped to break up a long night shift like nothing else could. That memory had his smile growing.

The grin turned to longing as he got lost in his thoughts again. He registered the goodbyes and friendly smiles as he wound his way through the hallways to the side entrance he always used. The sun was just beginning its day as he passed by the floor to ceiling windows.

His mind centered on the recurring daydream that took up residence in his head during his downtime. It was a longtime fantasy, one that held him through the lonely times when he'd been in the middle of BFE on deployment and separated from Derek for months on end. He'd never shared this with anyone, not even Derek. But the dream had to do with beachside property, loads of sun, big buckets full of beer, and him and Derek, naked in the surf. Inappropriate thoughts flooded his brain as they always seemed to do when he focused on Derek. But damn, his lover sure would look good wearing nothing but sand and that sexy grin.

His cheeks heated and his cock started to plump just as his phone vibrated, causing his steps to falter. He pulled it from his pocket and smiled as he looked down at the blinking screen. On a whim, trying for something out of character, he'd sent Derek a quick text that contained only a heart emoji. Justin was still flying high from the tryst they'd shared earlier. He wanted to let Derek know he was thinking about him and what they'd done in the old supply closet. Justin hurriedly opened the text.

"*Where are you?*" Derek texted. Justin was just about to the side door exit when he stopped and stepped aside, away from the foot traffic in the busy hall, while he responded.

"*Leaving, where are you? Did you get the dog food?*" Justin texted.

"*I'm waiting on you. We need to talk this morning.*" Justin read the words. His heart plunged as he read them again. Okay, that didn't sound good.

"*What about?*" he quickly typed back.

"*Us. Can you meet me at home real quick? I need to*

see my aunt afterward." What did *us* mean? The happy feelings of a minute ago faded as Derek's recent attitude resurfaced. They'd been perfectly in sync during their time spent in the closet less than two hours ago. The sadness Derek carried around the last couple of weeks had vanished during those few short minutes. He thought the closet sex might have made things better. What had happened since then to require a talk?

"*Just tell me,*" Justin finally typed. His heart hammered in his chest. Why did this feel like he was being dumped? This had been his biggest fear since they first met. Okay, not since they first met, but from when he realized Derek wanted more than just a one-night stand. He'd hidden behind the military and he'd let that restrict them, always worrying when Derek would eventually get sick of him and that lifestyle. He shockingly never had, but the truth that he'd never shared was that he always felt unworthy. Justin loved Derek. There was no doubt about that. Derek was his world. But he'd felt that the relationship he had with Derek was a pipedream. Something that could all be ripped away if he got too complacent. All those years in the military, he had waited for the shoe to drop and Derek to find someone better suited for him. He didn't know why because the man had never once given him a reason to feel anything but secure. It was just his own fucked up way of thinking that made him feel undeserving. Now that he'd let his guard down and allowed himself to envision their long life together, Derek was finally going to let him go?

Hell, he could feel his safeguards slipping back in place. At some point, Dr. Derek Babineaux would see him for what he was—an average, boring guy who was way too reserved. He almost didn't want to read the next text when it came through. He knew what was coming, and those few seconds were some of the longest of his life. He steeled his heart and forced the text open when it came.

"I stayed late after work. I'm tired of us hiding our relationship. I'm about to hit send on the paperwork Human Resources needs that shows we're together. I thought I should ask you first, but I don't want you to talk

me out of it." Justin dropped his head back on the glass and closed his eyes, relief flooded him. Thank heaven, it wasn't what he thought. Quite the opposite, but still bad. How did he feel about this?

He refused to overthink. He'd just faced the dire reality of losing Derek, and he never wanted to do that again. He needed to man-up and make sure that never happened, instead of waiting day by day for the inevitable. "*Push send. What do I need to do?*"

"*It's sent. They'll send you something to fill out. Thank you for this.*"

"*I love you—you don't have to thank me. I want this.*" Blinding relief flooded him. He quickly typed a second message, knowing there was no turning back after HR got involved. "*Are you sure I'm what you want?*"

"*Never more sure in my life. And since we've taken that step, I want you to go meet my aunt this morning and I want to meet your parents tonight. It's time to start living the life we've talked about.*" Derek replied a few seconds later.

How many times could his heart pound out of his chest in one day? Could he really do all this? *Yes, it's way past time,* echoed through his mind. Derek knew all the negative things about him and yet he still stuck around.

"*Okay, where are you?*" Justin finally typed back.

"*If I'd have known it was that easy, I would have taken you to the closet sooner. Can you meet me at the front of the ER? I need to close some things up.*"

"*Wait there for me. I'm across the campus.*" Justin refused to overanalyze and decided to just accept the relief he felt. He turned, retracing his steps back to the emergency room. The uncertainty faded as he saw Derek standing closer to the front desk than the front doors. He was talking to someone, smiling and laughing. As Justin got closer, he could see it was one of the females he seemed to talk to quite a bit.

He came to a stop right in front of Derek. He got that smile he loved the most as the conversation finished and he stood there waiting. "Amanda, meet Justin, my boyfriend."

Justin nodded at the shocked face staring back at him. Derek laughed and extended a hand toward the door, but Justin didn't walk in front of him. Instead he reached out, took his hand, and intertwined their fingers together. Derek hesitated for a second, but he quickly caught up and wrapped his fingers around Justin's.

"That's new." Derek's smile was bigger than he ever remembered.

"I love you," Justin whispered so quietly he wondered if Derek had even heard him.

"I love you, too," Derek said a little louder and winked at Justin before he turned toward the door. Justin was a little slower to follow. The clicking sounds behind him had him turning back to the nurses' station. Two nurses from the night shift were still there, and one had her cellphone camera out, snapping a picture in his direction. That completely confused him.

"Come on, Romeo. It's gonna sink in that you're truly off the market, and they'll turn into vultures. Besides, you need your game face on to meet my aunt. She's going to be so angry we hid this from her for so long."

Justin stayed quiet, letting the moment settle inside him. The thought of Aunt Vera's scolding scared him more than everyone finding out about them. His first public display hadn't destroyed him. No one jumped out of the woodwork to point a finger at him. The world hadn't opened up and swallowed him whole. Derek went through the automatic doors first and he followed. About twenty steps outside the door, he felt a bump at his shoulder.

"I'm not complaining, but you might be cutting off the circulation to my fingers," Derek said teasingly. Justin realized he had the death grip on Derek's hand.

"Sorry," he loosened his hold, but Derek hung on tight.

"Not too far away. I like you here. Thank you. I was afraid this might not ever happen," Derek said nonchalantly as they continued walking, bypassing all the cabs.

"Did you really file paperwork with HR?" Justin asked.

"I did. You said to push send." Uncertainty filled Derek's voice, and he hated he put that look there yet again.

"I'll turn mine in tonight," Justin stated, smiling as the uncertainty faded and Derek's thumb caressed his hand. He supposed that meant he approved of the answer. "I'm gonna admit, your aunt scares me a little bit."

"Yeah, me too. She lives a couple of blocks up. We can have breakfast and walk the blocks. She'll be up and dressed by the time we get there. Thank you for going with me," Derek said again and lifted their joined hands.

"It feels good," he offered as they came to the first red light on the block.

"I agree, real good." Derek leaned in, meeting him more than halfway with puckered lips. Justin watched those dancing green eyes challenge him.

"It's like a Band-Aid," Derek teased, leaning a little farther in. Justin manned-up and slightly extended for the kiss. It was quick and fast, but the warmth in his cheeks flared. "You've made me a very happy man this morning. Your family next?"

"Baby steps. We'll get our game plan in place where they're concerned this afternoon."

"I'll take what I can get as long as we throw marriage into the mix." Derek waggled his eyebrows at him. What? Where had marriage ever come from? That was completely new, but as the idea settled over him, he found he really liked it. Trying to hide his excitement, he fished his sunglasses from his hoodie pocket and slid them in place as they reached the corner.

"I'll talk marriage if you talk beachfront property." The light changed and he stepped out into the crosswalk.

"Beachfront property?" Derek questioned, falling in step beside him.

"Yeah, I bet you look really good wearing nothing but sand." They walked side by side, hand in hand, into the small cafe.

The End

To meet Derek's friend, Tristan Wilder, look for his book Secret - Now Available

BONUS CONTENT

DEREK MEETS JUSTIN

The hard beat of the bass echoed off the walls of the small venue as Derek took a seat at the bar and signaled the bartender for a new drink. The loud music made it almost impossible to carry on any kind of conversation with his good friend Tristan Wilder, who sat beside him, disinterestedly chomping on the ice from the glass he held. They were the only two males in the place not partaking in the current night's activities. Neither so much as glanced toward the hired female strippers who were dancing freely around the crowd of partygoers at the bachelor party.

A fresh cocktail was pushed in his direction; he took it, nodding his approval before lifting the glass to his lips. Derek watched closely as the dark-haired bartender quickly and efficiently poured drinks for the attendees. He wasn't all that certain such a small private party should produce that much revelry, but clearly the partygoers weren't privy to his train of thought. They were in New Orleans after all, and as usual, people discarded their inhibitions.

NOLA had a colorful reputation; they didn't call it the Big Easy for nothing. And it was common knowledge—if it could be had, you could get it on Bourbon Street. Derek had tested that piece of information firsthand. It was why he'd chosen emergency medicine over any other specialty available. Without question, at the current rate this gathering was going, someone in his party would be hitting the ER tonight.

"You sure know how to throw a party," Derek shouted toward Tristan who spun around on his barstool and anchored both elbows on the bar before leaning back.

"Yeah, it should make for an interesting trip home tomorrow," Tristan yelled his reply, giving a little smirk. Derek busted out laughing at Tristan's comment. Almost everyone at the party was completely trashed. Even he had drunk a little too much. The turbulence of a flight, along with the unsteady stomach of a hangover, never made for an ideal situation.

"Thanks for coming out tonight!" Tristan hollered right about the time a song hit its climax and made it impossible to hear the guy. Derek moved in closer to catch a little of what Tristan was saying. That didn't work, so Derek turned his head, so that his ear was closer to Tristan's mouth, hoping the change in position would drown out some of the noise. That move had him facing out the front window of the bar where he could see the busy street on the other side of the glass. Derek took in the large group of people meandering on the sidewalk in front of the nightclub, his eyes drifting from person to person until his gaze landed on a trim, tanned, muscular form crossing the street. The guy walked briskly and kept his head down as he stepped up onto the sidewalk. Derek watched as the guy stopped, pausing briefly before turning to look back across the street toward the direction he'd just come. Derek wondered if he might be waiting for someone. The best Derek could tell, the guy was alone. After a few seconds, the mystery man finally turned his head toward the window, as if he could feel the weight of Derek's gaze. At that moment Derek's body instantly went on notice and his dick fucking jumped to attention. He was gorgeous! There was no way the guy could see Derek from this angle, but from where Derek sat it was as if the handsome man's eyes bore right through the glass and spoke to his soul. He was ruggedly good-looking with a sexy hot, close-cropped military haircut. Derek was off his chair in a flash, eyes stayed riveted to the man outside as he hurried through the bar, hoping to intercept him. Derek picked up his pace and jogged toward the front doors when the gorgeous guy was out of the range of the window.

Derek shoved the bar door open, the humid night air hit him as he glanced around the overly crowded Bourbon street in search of his mystery man. He took off jogging, franticly scanning the mass of people until he saw the guy a short distance ahead. He slowed, walking a couple of steps behind the man and admiring the view. The guy was tall, at least as tall as Derek, and well-defined, that perfect bubble butt swaying with each step he took. When did wearing walking shorts, a T-shirt, and flip-flops become sexy as hell?

Quickly adjusting the hard-on tightening his jeans, Derek quickened his pace, sidling up next to the guy, matching his stride.

"Hey." He had more than his fair share of liquor, and his word sounded a little slurred so he stopped talking right there, not attempting to say anything more. Admittedly not his smoothest moment.

"Hey?" the guy replied, turning to look at him, confusion twisting his face. But when their gazes met, Derek pretty much lost his mind. He couldn't look away and he couldn't speak. His steps faltered, tripping on a dip in the sidewalk, but seconds before he hit the pavement, a powerful set of arms hauled him forward and then continued to draw him in to a rather enticing set of pecs. *Oh, fuck me!*

Derek should have been embarrassed over his momentary blunder, but he wasn't. Instead he moved fully into the sexy man's hold, leaning in to smell his cologne. Damn, this guy smelled as delicious as he looked. His dick twitched in agreement.

~~~

Fuck, why was it so hard for Justin to talk, to pick someone up? It had been far too long, and he swore he was developing callouses on his palm from all the self-love he'd been engaging in lately. Justin forced himself to keep moving forward. The never-ending mental criticism and his lack of action had him shaking his head. What the fuck had he been thinking? That guy had been interested in him, but he let him pass right by. That totally defeated his sole purpose of hitting the town tonight, which was to get laid at least once before he left. He was never going to get any if he didn't get better at his come-ons.

"Hey." At first Justin hadn't turned his head, but something about the deeply cultured Southern tone made him want to, if for nothing more than the visual. He was certain whoever had spoken in that husky voice had to
~~~

be hot. A heartbeat or two passed before he finally gave in to curiosity. He turned his head, and his gaze locked with the most breathtaking eyes he'd ever seen. He couldn't form a coherent thought for several seconds. It took one step, then two for him to respond.

"Hey?" he managed to mumble. Not that his *hey* could be considered well thought out by any means, but for the first time in his life, it wasn't the fear of speaking that held his tongue. What kept him silent was his breath being sucked from his body. Those emerald eyes pierced his soul, striking him dumb. His normal reaction time slowed. He watched as his dream guy stumbled and started to fall forward. It took a second for his brain to catch up and for him to reach out before the handsome blond met the pavement.

Hands gripped his T-shirt and a solid chest bumped into his. He did a small what probably looked like a dance move, flipping himself a half turn to keep them both on their feet. An arm locked around his waist. It took a minute or two more for him to realize he wasn't being held to maintain balance. That was already taken care of. Instead, he felt the scrape of stubble against his neck and a nice hard dick rubbing against his, the need matching his own. The faint smell of alcohol drifted on the air as the guy leaned back without lessening his hold and looked him in the eyes.

Don't blow this, he mentally warned himself.

"Thank you for rescuing me. My very own prince charming. Are you here alone tonight?" The guy's grin mesmerized Justin.

"Yeah." Was his brilliant response. But in his defense, his tongue was still tied.

"My place's close. You interested?" Justin was silent as his heart picked up a beat. It was the guy's eyes, among other things, that totally drew him in.

"Yeah," he finally muttered, dropping his gaze from the intense stare to the guy's full lips. Ah fuck, they were full and pouty, hot as hell lips. "Are you one of those male models?"

For the first time in too many years, Justin spoke without thinking. Heat rushed to his cheeks at what he'd just asked, but all those blond-haired, green-eyed models were just what summer spread men's clothing stores looked for in their advertisements.

"Nah, although I did have a short-lived gig at the local Abercrombie in the mall when I was younger. But I gave it all up to become a doctor. Dr. Derek Babineaux."

"Justin," was the only thing he could come up with.

"Here on leave?"

"Yeah," he answered. Maybe he was coming off as the strong brooding type. But he seriously doubted it. Someone bumped him from behind, knocking him forward, breaking the hold he had on the hot doctor. He didn't get too far away before a hand snaked out and gripped his forearm, drawing him out of the flow of traffic they'd been holding up.

"I live about a block away, want to follow me?"

Man, did he ever.

~~~
~~~

"This way. I just need to text my buddy and let 'em know I'm gone for the night." Derek walked down the hall toward his apartment. He pulled his phone from his back pocket and tried hard to concentrate on typing the few quick words and not on the hottie following behind him. He sent a quick message to Tristan apologizing for ditching his party before digging out his key and unlocking the front door. He went against his natural manners of letting Justin walk in before him and pushed open the door, dropping his phone and his keys on the inside entry table. He walked quickly through the living room, grabbing a jacket off the sofa and a shirt off the chair, hoping to hide his clutter.

"Nice place," Justin said, standing in the space between the entryway and the beginning of the living room. Derek bundled the clothes and grabbed some papers spread out across the table and quickly dumped them in a side closet before turning back.

"Thanks. Come in. Want a drink?" Derek asked. He made his way quickly around the living room, turning on the side table lamps. With each flip of a switch, the dark room lit up a little more, revealing just how gorgeous Justin truly was. He studied Justin closely. Full lips and wide-set eyes were the first thing he'd been drawn to. But as he looked closer, he noticed the upturned, inviting lift at the corner of his lips, the slight crook in his nose, how his thick dark lashes made his golden eyes stand out against his olive skin.

The guy's hair was a genuine auburn, the front left a little longer with the sides almost shaved. Justin was deeply tanned, completely void of freckles, well, the parts he could see anyway, which was interesting considering the color of his hair. He had strong wide shoulders, and to top it all off, a sexy masculine voice that Derek couldn't wait to hear moaning his name. Fuck, the heated look in the guy's eyes alone had him almost coming in his jeans. The more the guy watched him, the more Derek wanted him. Derek moved to turn on the last lamp, keeping his eyes on Justin. He missed a step and rammed his damn toe against the leg of the end table.

"Damn it," he muttered, reaching out to grab the lamp before it bit the dust. "I'm not usually this clumsy, honest." He glanced up to give Justin a grin. The guy gave a slight nod but didn't say anything. He stayed rooted in his spot by the door, his fingers tucked in his front pockets as his attention moved to the back of the room. Derek followed the direction of his eyes and didn't notice anything out of place. Maybe Justin was just being nice, not wanting to acknowledge his fumble. Good-looking and a gentleman too? He liked that. "How about a drink?"

"Sure." It wasn't much to go on. Justin clearly wasn't much of a talker. Derek headed to the bar and poured a couple of shots before looking over his shoulder. Justin was back to studying him again. His body amped-up another notch under the intense scrutiny. Fuck, he liked being the center of Justin's attention way too much.

"Go ahead and make yourself at home." Derek watched Justin move across the room. The strut was just as sexy to watch from the front as it had been from the back. When Justin got within reach, he handed him the shot glass before picking up his own and raising it for a toast. "To a memorable evening."

Justin lifted the drink and clanked the edge of his glass against Derek's before finishing the double in one gulp. The guy barely winced as he tossed back the shot. Derek followed suit and downed his while still holding Justin's gaze. Justin's eye's dropped to his Adam's apple as the liquid blazed down his throat like fire. After he finished, he slammed the glass down on the bar as the familiar warmth began to spread throughout his body.

Derek had planned to move in for the kiss, but held back, giving the guy room. He slid the bottle toward Justin who was clearly interested in what he was seeing, but might need a little more liquid courage to drive him on. Perhaps that meant newly out? Or maybe he was just being reserved. Who knew? Derek waited as Justin refilled both the glasses to the rim. Derek downed his as quickly as Justin.

Drunk sex was fun, but Derek could sense a sexually spiritual awakening coming his way, and he wanted to be sober enough to commit every detail to memory. After taking the glass from Justin, he discarded it on the granite counter. Time to move things along. He grabbed the bottle off the bar and brought it to his lips, filling his mouth with the amber liquid before moving in. Justin opened for him under the press of his lips. The heat of the alcohol and the feel of Justin's tongue hungrily probing his mouth was a heady mix, something he could grow accustomed to.

Their tongues twisted and mingled as they explored each other's mouths. Powerful bodies, pliant, melded into the other. Breaking from the kiss to catch his breath, Derek couldn't remember a time where he'd been so turned on, so completely needy. Need couldn't even begin to describe the feeling coursing through his body.

Derek pulled back, searching for any hesitancy on Justin's part and found none. He reached for the guy's T-shirt and brought it up and over Justin's head, tossing it aside. His eyes slid up and down Justin's form, his mouth watering at all that male flesh waiting to be explored. Erotic images filled his head. Justin must have keyed in on his carnal thoughts and wanted the same because the corners of his mouth turned up in a knowing grin.

"You're perfect." Derek's fingertips lightly traced the solid ridges of Justin's abs.

"And I want you in me so fucking bad," Justin replied.

"That can be arrang—" Before Derek could finish his sentence, eager fingers slid into his hair as Justin's mouth came crashing down on his. The kiss was urgent and raw, heated and reckless. Hunger built quickly as their tongues swirled and danced.

He freed Justin's cock from the man's shorts and fondled the hard span as he worked to push the material down and off his hips. Justin fumbled with Derek's buttons. He broke from the kiss only to help, hurriedly ridding himself of the offending material. They shed their clothing quickly, leaving it where it fell. Their cocks rubbed together with every movement, causing a low moan to escape from Derek's lips. Justin's hands were on him immediately, searching, franticly exploring every needy inch. Derek sucked in a breath when Justin's fingers circled his length and began stroking him.

Derek broke from the kiss and licked a path from Justin's perfect jaw, along the five o'clock shadow, to the shell of his ear. "So fucking hot."

He sucked at the soft skin on Justin's neck, loving the feel of Justin's firm grip sliding up and down his shaft. Using his weight, he pressed Justin against the wall, holding him there. He kissed along his collarbone and down his chest, bending his head to take Justin's nipple between his teeth before swirling his tongue around the tightening bud. The steady strokes on his dick faltered, and he couldn't help smiling to himself when Justin moaned. More. He wanted to hear more of those little sounds, and he wanted to taste more of this gorgeous man. He started to lower himself to his knees.

"I won't last if you suck me." Justin's hands moved to his face, clasping his cheeks between palms, halting his movement. "I need to be fucked."

"And you will be," he promised, smoothing his hands up Justin's side as he rose. His palms skated over the perfect roundness of Justin's ass. Derek squeezed, kneading the firm round globes. He secured his hands under Justin's ass and lifted. Justin didn't hesitate and wrapped his legs around him in one powerful, fluid motion. Their lips melded together. The feel of Justin's naked skin grinding against his own hardened flesh sent waves of desire coursing through his body, settling heavily in his balls.

He carried Justin down the hallway into the bedroom and tumbled them onto the mattress, Justin half on him, half on the bed as he pulled him into a needy embrace. Their mouths fused together, caressing and tasting. The scent of their mingled arousal, heady and thick, filled the room.

"I'm gonna fuck you so hard you won't ever forget me." Derek growled against Justin's mouth.

"Please," Justin replied.

Derek sat up and grabbed for the package of condoms and bottle of lube he kept in the nightstand, tossing them on the bed. Justin moved toward the center of the mattress and pulled the pillows toward him, using them to prop himself up. His thick cock lay firm and strong against his belly. Derek leisurely took in the sight of the gorgeous man laid out in front of him and all that tempting flesh waiting to be touched.

"Tell me what you like, Justin. No, better yet, show me." There wasn't any hesitation as Justin lowered his hand and began stroking that beautiful thick cock. *Holy hell! That's hot*. Maybe the guy wasn't so shy after all.

"Shit, you've got me so hard just watching you." He groaned as Justin brought those long fingers to his lips and sucked them in. Derek had a feeling he was about to get harder when Justin drew his legs up and back toward his chest and spread his thighs wide. Derek couldn't keep his hands off his own leaking cock as Justin shamelessly pleasured himself.

Those captivating eyes held him in place, inviting him to watch as Justin's finger disappeared deep into his ass. No, there wasn't one bit of shame in this guy's game as he fingered his smooth hole. Justin continued to stare at him, eyes hooded, lips parted as he fucked himself with his fingers. Derek's fist tightened on his own cock as he watched Justin's digits slide in and out of his body.

"Fuck! I could watch you all night." Derek stroked his leaking cock with one hand and reached forward with the other to smooth his palm up the inside of Justin's thigh. "But I'm not going to." Leaning in, he pressed his mouth to Justin's and kissed him, long and slow. Justin's lips were firm yet pliable beneath his. He sucked Justin's bottom lip into his mouth, nipping before swiping his tongue across the fullness. Derek's need to replace Justin's fingers with his own won out. Pulling back from the kiss, he quit stroking himself, grasped Justin's wrist and removed Justin's fingers. Watching the guy fuck himself was a huge turn-on, but he really wanted to be the one pleasuring Justin. Derek released Justin's wrist, picked up the lube and coated his fingers with the cool slick liquid before getting into a better position.

He circled the rim of Justin's ass with his fingertip before pushing his digit inside. Justin's long fingers gripped the comforter, his other hand remained on his dick, slowly stroking himself as Derek breached him.

Derek pumped his finger in and out, enjoying the tight grip of Justin's clenching channel. When Derek felt the muscle relax, he added a second finger, fucking Justin faster before pulling out and pressing in with his thumb to massage the soft skin around Justin's entrance. Justin squirmed.

"Derek, please." Justin's voice sounded husky with need.

Without any hesitation, Derek picked up the foil package and used his teeth to open it before rolling the condom down his aching cock. After coating his length and fingers with lube, he fitted himself into the space between Justin's spread thighs. He teased his dick along the crevice of Justin's ass, enjoying the glide against his sensitive prick.

"Gonna fuck you now." Derek stared down into blue eyes and pushed slowly into that snug opening. His cock head pressed past the taut ring of muscle and slid partway inside. Justin's constricting warmth engulfed him, gripping him with the sweetest of pressures. Derek had to fight to keep from doing what he really wanted to do—

pound mindlessly into that welcoming heat. He gritted his teeth to help combat the urge.

"God, you're so tight. You feel so good," he panted. Justin looked up at him, those bright eyes filled with lust. He held his position, not moving, as he allowed Justin's body time to adjust. The fight for control of his body in that moment was unlike anything he'd ever experienced before. This guy was rattling him to the core, tilting his world on its axis.

Derek placed his hands on either side of Justin's head. Lowering his body, he sank into Justin, sliding deeper, inch by inch until his balls pressed firmly against Justin's ass. Justin's body clenched around him.

"You feel too good." His need to thrust overwhelmed him. Self-control was a futile thought. "Fuck! Your ass is squeezing me so tight, gotta move now."

"Move, don't hold back on my account. Fuck me, Derek." Justin moaned and circled his hips.

"Gonna bury myself so deep in you." Derek reared back and thrust inside. Justin gasped and ground against him. He pulled slowly out until only the tip remained then pushed back in, trying to get as deep as he could inside this man.

"Yes, harder," Justin pleaded and wrapped those long muscular legs around his waist; the heels digging into his ass spurred him on. They rocked together for what seemed like forever, lost in the pleasure building and growing as their bodies moved in perfect rhythm. He changed his angle, trying to bury himself deeper in Justin's heat. Justin threw his head back, baring his neck.

"Ahhga, Derek…shit! Yes, oh god, yes!" His change of position caused Justin to shudder. He took advantage of that bit of knowledge and pounded into him, hitting that spot over and over. His arms shook, his legs weakened, and his thrusts became even more uncoordinated with every word that escaped Justin's lips. He was going to come if Justin kept it up. Usually he loved a loud vocal partner, but with this guy, it was such a turn on that he needed to do something to regain his composure and prolong things. He didn't want it to end. Derek dipped his head and captured Justin's mouth, stopping his words with a fervent kiss.

That kiss was the wrong move, because Justin was too responsive. The pressure burned in his spine, his balls ached, growing heavy with his seed and the need for release. He had thought that he could prolong his orgasm, but the need to come was just too overpowering. Caught between losing himself in pleasure and giving in to the inevitable, he pumped mindlessly into Justin's body.

"Fuck! So good." He pulled out and slammed back in a few more times, before tunneling his arm under Justin's neck and drawing him closer. He rested more of his weight on his forearm as he slid a hand between their sweat-slickened bodies to take hold of Justin's cock and stroke him.

"Derek…yes!" Justin panted against his mouth. The sting of nails scraping down his back had his hips double timing. Justin's body tensed, his cock twitched, and hot come spilled over his fingers as his lover's ass clamped down hard around his dick.

"Justin," he whispered. His vision went dark, and his breath caught in his throat as he tumbled over the edge, filling the condom with one final mind-blowing thrust.

His arms and legs gave out, and he collapsed on top of Justin. Their breathing settled and the beating of their hearts slowed, taking on the same rhythm. Derek didn't want to move. Strangely enough, he had a feeling that Justin felt the same. He lifted his head, opening his eyes, and found Justin smiling up at him.

"That's exactly what the doctor ordered." Justin's fingers combed through his hair as he stretched out beneath him, a boyish after-sex grin still plastered on that handsome face.

"Glad I could be of service. And in your case, I might even be willing to make house calls," he chuckled and kissed the tip of Justin's nose.

"I could get spoiled to that particular kind of service, Dr. Babineaux." Something flashed in Justin's eyes, but vanished just as quickly.

"Stay the night?" It wasn't the words that caught him off guard, what caught him off guard was the ease in which he'd asked that question. This was unfamiliar territory. Spending the night had always been off limits, a rule he'd set long ago and followed closely. But tonight had been altogether different, and he didn't give a shit about his rules. He'd never felt as complete as he did in this moment. From the first time he laid eyes on Justin, he knew without a doubt this man was different than all the others and he wasn't about to let him get away.

~~~

The crisp, cool sheets tangled around Justin's legs as something stirred him awake. He fought to stay asleep, reminding himself that he was on leave and didn't have to be up at the butt crack of dawn. He was still a bit hung over from all the drinks last night but not enough that his body wasn't screaming for release. Justin thought about the previous night, and just the thought of the things Derek had done to him brought a silly grin to his face. Stretching his body out, he ignored the catch in his back and pushed the blankets low as he reached down and
~~~

grasped his rigid dick. He kept his eyes closed as he brought the sexy doctor's image to mind. Damn, Derek had known exactly what he needed and when to give it.

That last thought caused his belly to do a little flip. Perhaps he'd fallen a little harder for the doctor than he was willing to admit. The sex had been off the charts hot. Derek was undeniably a skilled lover; his ass wasn't even protesting this morning. The guy had been so intuitive and tender with him. Knowing just how to pleasure him as if they'd been lovers for years. Sex had never been that earth-shattering before. A one-night stand was all he had set out in search of when he'd headed down to Bourbon Street. A quick fuck, an easy release, nothing more. But Dr. Derek Babineaux had penetrated his well laid defenses, and in one night, had him craving so much more.

Giving himself a slow tug, he reached low with his free hand and fondled his sac, just the way Derek had. The feeling was too much. His hips arched forward, driving his hard length deeper into his fist. Derek's handsome face came to mind. The intense need in his eyes, his scent, the way he lowered his head, giving a small smile seconds before those full, firm lips made contact with his. He worked himself root to tip and back again, using his thumb to spread the slick pre-come around the head of his dick. His breathing picked up just thinking about that sexy man in the middle of one of his orgasms.

Justin pumped faster, gripping his cock more firmly as he fucked his fist, giving into the hot fantasy of making love to Derek Babineaux. Last night had given him plenty of memories to call up for days or even months to come. He bit his bottom lip and thought about the way Derek's powerful body had felt pounding…

"God, you're sexy as hell," he heard whispered.

Fuck! Justin's hand stilled immediately, and his eyes popped open. His hips, though, seemed to have a mind of their own, thrusting forward in search of the orgasm that was so very close. He slowly turned his head toward the direction of that sexy voice.

Derek's brow lifted and the corner of his mouth curled into a smirk. "Were you thinking of me?" *Fucking shit, shit, shit! Dammit!* He'd been caught red-handed. That knowing smirk on Derek's handsome face threatened to send him over the edge. He should really let go of his dick before he embarrassed himself even more. Last night he'd pleasured himself for Derek, but that was different; he'd had plenty to drink and he didn't want to refuse the sexy doctor's request.

Derek's sleep-reddened eyes slowly moved to Justin's hand. God, he felt stupid. How in the hell had he forgotten he spent the night? Probably because he never stayed all night with anyone. Derek had fucked him so well and thoroughly he'd broken his own rules. At this moment, he didn't know whether he should be more mortified or turned the fuck on. The look in Derek's eyes suggested the latter.

"Please don't stop on my account. I'm rather enjoying the show." Derek's voice was smooth and sensual, sliding over his body like fine silk.

The familiar arousal had already started to build in his spine, and he wanted nothing more than to please Derek. Still unsure of what he should do in this situation, he quickly squeezed his dick at the root hard enough to derail his orgasm. Closing his eyes, he willed himself to calm down. Last night he'd had the handsome doctor every which way; was it rude to act so eager this morning? Justin took a deep breath and exhaled slowly.

"Here, let me." His hips arched forward of their own accord when Derek's strong, warm hand replaced his and began working him with long, hard strokes. Justin's mind reeled from embarrassment, but it seemed his body was totally on board with Derek's plan.

Derek's rhythm was maddening, and the pressure on his cock was perfect, just the way he liked it.

"Tell me who were you thinking about?" Derek's voice startled him back to reality.

He opened his eyes and looked straight at Derek. "You," he answered honestly. Yes, he was still humiliated he'd been caught jacking-off, but he wouldn't deny his attraction to the handsome man.

"Good answer," Derek said before he bent forward and took Justin's full length into that warm wet mouth.

THE MORNING AFTER

The doorbell rang. Derek grabbed his wallet and the stack of loose bills off the nightstand, thumbing through the money, searching for the proper tip as he headed for the door. He'd ordered breakfast and coffee from the deli downstairs, offering extra money to get it delivered quickly. It seemed to work. Justin was still in the bathroom, which gave him a little more time to figure out the best way to keep the guy in the apartment. He hoped to make this more than a one-night stand.

Completely out of his usual character, he didn't normally do things like this. Actually, no, come to think of it, he never did things like this. He couldn't quite put his finger on what exactly made Justin different, but he honestly couldn't get the guy out of his system. He didn't want to let him go. Now his life's mission was to find out everything he could about this amazing guy that stumbled into his life.

Derek went through the process of paying before quickly laying out the beignets and kolaches along with a few other pastries he'd had brought up. He took two coffee cups from the holder and spread the creamers out next to the small coffee carafe, wanting everything to be perfect. As a last minute thought, he grabbed some napkins and placed them next to the pastries.

"Hey," Justin said from behind him, and Derek jerked around to face him. He'd been lost in thought and hadn't heard his approach. "Did I take too long?"

"What? No, of course not. I had the deli downstairs bring up a little bit of everything they had. I wasn't sure what you liked." Derek took a step to the side to show the food he'd just set on the table.

"For me?" Justin asked, sounding a little shocked. A few steps away, he remained in place as he surveyed the pastries.

"Yeah?" Derek replied, not fully understanding why Justin sounded so unsure.

"Oh, okay." Only then did Justin move forward while continuing to look over the selection. "Can I just have any of these?"

"Of course. I got coffee, juice, and sodas too." Derek watched Justin closely. He wouldn't go so far as to say things had become awkward between them, but they definitely weren't as fluid as they had been last night.

"Really? You did this for me? Or is someone else coming over?" Justin asked inquisitively before taking a big bite out of a fruit-filled kolache.

"Yes. No. I mean I got them for you..." Confusion made Derek close his mouth and stop talking. Justin was derailing his planned conversation. Not on purpose, but apparently they weren't on the same wave length at all. He really wanted to spend as much time as he could with Justin. The guy intrigued him. He wanted to get to know him better. He obviously was going about this the wrong way. Perhaps the direct approach might work better. But what if Justin was only truly interested in a one-night stand? Damn, he hadn't been this nervous since the

MCAT. Probably the best thing to do would be to start over.

"You said you were on leave. I'm off a few days with no plans. Maybe we could spend that time together. I meant it when I told you I enjoyed spending time with you last night."

Justin didn't react. He swallowed that bite and just kept staring until he began worrying his bottom lip as if thoughtfully considering the answer to his question. "Okay, I'd like that. I just need to go home and take care of a few things."

"Sure. Bring a change of clothes when you come back." Justin nodded and then gave him a genuine smile. The smile reached his eyes and changed his already handsome face, making him even more endearing. "Good. That's settled. Do you like coffee? I have some soda and milk I think."

"A Dr. Pepper's good, if you have it." He made a mental note of Justin's choice of soda.

"I do, take a seat. I'll get it for you."

MOVING IN

Justin carried one of Derek's suitcases up the walkway to their brand new townhome. It was a nice place, something they'd picked out together a few weeks ago just after Derek landed the job in the local emergency room. Since then, they'd been caught up in a whirlwind of activity.

"Do you think that's the movers?" Derek asked, eyeing an eighteen-wheeler turning onto their street.

"They're right on time if it's them." He continued up the walkway, Derek moving a little faster, working his new key inside the front door. Derek stepped through first, holding the door open for him. Justin followed, barely making it through the opening before Derek slammed it shut in his wake.

Justin looked back at the door, then up at the light fixtures to see if anything might have been jarred out of place. Seconds later, Derek had him hooked around the waist, forcing him toward the entryway wall. Derek pressed him against the wall. Justin's breath hitched as Derek pinned him in place. Those piercing green eyes filled with need and concern. God, how he loved this man. Those fully fuckable lips mere inches away from his own. He would never grow tired of Derek, never. But he always had that lingering doubt in his head… Was what he doing enough? Had he asked too much of Derek? He tried so desperately to push aside his stupid unfounded fears and concentrate on how lucky he was. He shouldn't be so worried about the trivial shit. But he couldn't help it. There were so many ways this whole thing could crumble and leave Justin devastated and alone.

"Stop, Justin. You're too quiet. You're overthinking this. You always overthink things. We're good. I love you. You love me. Moving in together's the natural next step. It's no one else's business."

He relaxed a little. Derek caged him in against the wall and forced him to look deep into those beautiful eyes. Justin lifted his hands to Derek's waist holding him there. Derek's touch alone had always calmed him. Yes,

Derek knew him too well. Derek read his moods like a book, and it shouldn't surprise him he had honed in on his feelings today.

"You gave up a lot to move across the country and I…" Justin started, feeling guilt about everything Derek gave up for him. Derek's fingers pressed against his lips stopping his words.

"Stop it. What we have doesn't come along very often. I'm not letting you go, not for any reason and especially not because you doubt yourself. You'll be enough for me, you'll always be enough for me, I promise. You have to stop worrying about that. I love you, Justin Delacroix."

"I don't know if I can. I'm afraid everything'll be ripped away." Justin spoke honestly.

"Then focus on believing in me. I'm here because there's no place else I want to be and I'm more than willing to play by your rules." The doorbell rang but Derek didn't move, his powerful body still holding him in place, pressing him tightly against the wall. Derek stayed there right in Justin's face. The weight of his body was more a calming comfort than an unwelcomed pressure. “Now tell me you love me and you’re glad I’m here.”

“I’m sorry you have to hide.” Derek rolled his eyes at him. The eye rolling had become more prevalent lately, and somehow the showiness of it all managed to drive the last bit of lingering uncertainty from his thoughts.

“Not what I said.” The doorbell rang again.

“I am glad you’re here. I’ve been excited to start our life. It’s just today that got me spooked.” There he said it. Derek smiled and kissed him quickly on the lips.

“Let’s get this unloaded and have dinner ordered in. I’ve missed you and I can’t wait to show you how much. I promise you everything’ll work out.” Derek’s eyes never left his as he released his hold and moved toward the front door. Justin nodded then returned Derek’s smile, feeling much more settled. Derek masterfully read his moods and easily calmed him down. The door opened, and Justin quickly moved the suitcases out of the way, allowing the movers to bring the first load in.

MEETING AUNT VERA

Justin trailed behind as Derek took the steps up to the luxury home. He'd met Derek's Aunt Vera earlier in the evening when he'd drawn her blood in the ER. The bold declarations he'd made when leaving the hospital began to fade as he looked around the well-established gated community. Insecurity started to nudge its way into his well laid plans of being open and fully out as a couple. He knew this area, having driven past this neighborhood, even this house, many times throughout his life. When he was a kid, he'd dreamed of birthday parties, secret treehouses, and what wondrous presents awaited the children of this neighborhood on Christmas morning. As he grew older, he'd resented the show of wealth and the perfect life he didn't have.

Since he'd moved back to New Orleans, this neighborhood represented everything he wasn't and constantly reminded him of the major differences between him and the man he loved. These people never questioned where the money came from to pay their electric bills. Yet keeping the lights on was a conversation his parents had every single month throughout his entire childhood. He didn't fit here.

"Getting cold feet?" Derek asked, staring at him over his shoulder. He hadn't realized how much distance he'd allowed between them. He stood at the base of the porch steps while Derek had made it to the top and reached for the doorbell. Derek paused his movements as worry crossed his brow. That expression had Justin picking up his pace. There was no way he was going back there again. He double-timed it up the remaining few steps, hopefully giving the impression of having more courage than he really possessed. Justin reached out and pressed the doorbell.

"Do I look okay? Maybe I should've showered first," he said, nervously running his palm over the front of his close-cropped hair, making sure it laid the way it should.

"You look fine like always." Derek reached out and took his hand, intertwining their fingers. He heard the locks at the front door click. "Now let me handle this. That quiet thing you do should start now."

~~~

Derek hid the grin tugging at his lips as he turned toward the front door. Justin was nervous and trying so hard to keep that hidden. It was a sweet gesture, one he appreciated more than he ever thought possible. Maybe he should have pushed them out of their comfort zone a little sooner.

He suspected his Aunt Vera would be opening the front door herself. She had help, a full staff of workers employed every day inside her home, but she liked to do things herself then complain about paying for employees that offered no help. It was actually a huge part of every conversation they shared.

Derek squeezed Justin's hand in reassurance. He didn't miss it when Justin took an involuntary step backward. He chuckled a little and braced himself. He wanted to remember every reaction his aunt had when
~~~

she opened the door, and dear lord, he wasn't disappointed.

Aunt Vera stood there with her mouth open, ready with some comment she'd obviously forgotten as her eyes went from Derek to Justin then to their joined hands before traveling back to Derek. If he was correct, the last look she gave may have been approval before she hid that genuine expression with a scowl and took a step backward, opening the door wider.

"You have a lot of explaining to do, young man." He'd been dealing with her long enough to know that really meant "*Come in,*" so he gently began to guide Justin forward. His aunt's feisty attitude always made him smile.

"Yes, ma'am. But before we start all that, I want you to meet my boyfriend, Justin… Actually, he's more than just my boyfriend. Justin, this is my aunt, you met her tonight at the hospital." Derek gave a quick introduction while standing in the entryway. As she studied Justin, Derek reached over and shut the door she hadn't closed yet.

Of course Justin stayed quiet, he rarely spoke to anyone, but his aunt on the other hand was a different matter. She never shut up. The moment of silence wasn't lost on him as she said absolutely nothing in response to his statement. But the tears that filled her eyes were an unexpected surprise.

"You should have told me. I've been so worried about you." The tears spilled over and rolled down her face. She stepped forward, holding her arms out. Derek dropped Justin's hand and wrapped her in his arms, hugging her for several long minutes until he felt her body calm. The slap on his back and again on his arm had him loosening his hold as she pulled away. "You're in trouble for lying to me."

"Aunt Vera, I never lied. I simply omitted a few things. Justin was in the military, and we decided to keep this between us while he was still serving, to help protect him," Derek quickly explained.

"You're a military man?" Aunt Vera turned to Justin and asked. Of course that would impress her. She was most definitely in the age group where honor and integrity of a statesman meant something and Justin radiated those exact same qualities.

"Yes, ma'am, I was. I just got out," Justin answered. Derek eyed him closely. Justin looked a little shell-shocked. But who wouldn't, especially while attempting to answer his intimidating Aunt Vera's questions.

"Well, you have to stay through breakfast now and tell me everything you haven't. Was he the reason you moved across the country?" his aunt asked, turning away, making her way down a long hall toward the kitchen. Derek extended his hand, gesturing for Justin to go in front of him, but Justin just shook his head no, forcing Derek to follow first.

"Yes, ma'am," Derek finally answered, looking over his shoulder to make sure Justin hadn't bailed.

"I think I see a regularly scheduled Sunday brunch in your future for what you've put me through, Derek Babineaux," she scolded in the crusty tone she used. He just chuckled and turned again toward Justin.

"She can be pleasant, I promise," he said it loud enough for her to hear.

"Don't lie to him, Derek," Aunt Vera said, moving toward the dining room.

NOTHING BUT SAND

First class definitely has its perks, Justin thought to himself as he drained the last of his champagne. Nothing could beat the exceptional comfort or the impeccable service, at least that was what his handsome new husband Derek Babineaux always said. And he had to agree. A few years back, Derek had ditched flying the cramped confines of coach and introduced him to a finer way to fly. Since that day, they hadn't traveled any other way. Yet even with such a relaxing ride, Justin could feel himself growing antsy. They were hours into the flight, and he still had no idea where they were going or how much longer until they arrived at their final destination. Derek had insisted everything remain a secret.

Excitement bubbled in his stomach the moment Derek reached over and lowered the window blind, motioning for him to put his earbuds back in place. That meant he needed to up the volume on his phone and blare the music so he couldn't hear anything that might give the surprise away. He had to admit Derek had done an excellent job at keeping him in suspense since leaving their wedding reception however many hours ago.

Their wedding had been perfect, attended by family and friends. He couldn't have asked for more. Derek had played a big part in planning that too. The man knew what he wanted and made no bones about it, even the wedding planner had complimented his husband's extraordinary taste. His thoughts drifted over the past twenty-four hours, which brought a smile to his face. He was now a happily married man. God, he was so in love. It was crazy how much you could love someone, and he utterly adored Derek. Emotion welled in his heart, and he slid his hand across the armrest to thread his fingers with Derek's.

Derek glanced at him and, just like always, that heart-melting smile stole his breath. Funny how even after all this time together a thing as simple as a smile could cause such a physical reaction. He was indeed a very lucky man and currently being swept away on a honeymoon trip. A special getaway Derek had secretly spent months planning, not giving him any clue as to where they were going. Surprising him was something Derek had always enjoyed. Derek leaned closer, lifted the earbuds out of his ears, and whispered, "Get your blindfold ready. We're about to land, babe."

The blindfold had been another unexpected requirement given to him on the way to the airport. As silly as it seemed, Justin enjoyed playing along with his mister's little games. Now upon arrival, it seemed the same rules applied, and he would happily follow them.

They unloaded from the airplane, only making it to the end of the jet bridge before Derek placed a hand on his forearm to stop him, insisting he put on the blindfold. Like before, he repeated the process, lowering the blindfold securely in place, and again someone waited, ready to guide him out of the airport and help him inside the car. The experience was thrilling and awkward all at the same time. He took his seat in the car, Derek slid in beside him, and they were off once again. After what seemed like hours, the car slowed, finally coming to a stop. His heart started to race wildly in his chest as the anticipation grew. Hopefully this was the end of their journey, because he was ready to spend alone time with Derek.

"Stay here. Don't move. I'm going around to the other side of the car and you better not peek." Derek's voice carried a playful warning. Seconds later, his door opened, and Derek's steady hands slid around his upper body to help him out. He wobbled a little as he got out of the car and stretched to his full height. The long trip and the blindfold made things a little disorienting but he quickly steadied himself. Pausing a moment, he took in the sounds and smells around him. The warm breeze greeted him as a bird squawked overhead. Justin swore he also heard the sound of the ocean in the distance. Then it hit him, his honey remembered, and he couldn't help the grin spreading across his face. Derek must have planned their honeymoon at the beach, exactly like he'd wanted.

~~~
~~~

As excited as he was to explore the new property firsthand, Derek wanted to see Justin's reaction even more. He slid the blindfold off his husband's head and stood back to watch. He wasn't disappointed. Justin's eyes lit up. His handsome face transformed into something magical as his eyes took in the exclusive and magnificent beachfront bungalow. Derek finally turned his head to do the same.

"I hope you like it." Derek couldn't believe the beauty surrounding them. This was truly paradise. Blooming flowers and lush exotic plants blanketed the hillside. Stately palms swayed gently in the tropical breeze, bowing gracefully over sand white as snow. Bright turquoise water blended with the sky, giving the illusion of a never-ending horizon. Relief replaced apprehension; he'd done well. He'd been anxious since he hadn't been able to view the property himself, but in the end, it looked like the worry had been for nothing.

"I do. I love it!" Justin gave him a sweet kiss. "Thank you for remembering."

"You're welcome. Come on. Let's go inside." Derek smiled, tugging Justin along the sidewalk toward the front door.

"I still can't believe we're here. Is it private?" Justin asked, eagerly following him to the porch.

"This entire side of the island's exclusive," Derek answered, fishing the key out of his pocket before unlocking and opening the front door of the island home. An alarm beeped the minute they opened the door. He went to the wall device and entered the code he'd been given. "I was told we would be alone. Neither of our neighbors are here this weekend."

"Oh my god… It's huge! Derek, this is absolutely amazing," Justin exclaimed, moving into the living room, looking all around. The raised twenty foot ceiling and disappearing glass walls with deep lanais provided a breathtaking ocean view. A great place to just sit and soak up the island atmosphere.

"It's three bedrooms, but I'm told the master's the best part of the house. The room opens to a private beach with a small path leading to our own lagoon and waterfall." He watched as Justin turned back to the far windows, looking out over the spectacular ocean view.

"How long do we have it for?" Justin asked.

Ah, he didn't get it yet. Even better. Derek walked up behind Justin and wrapped his arms around his mister, kissing the back of his neck. He ran his nose up the side of Justin's neck.

"I bought it. It's ours. It's my wedding present to you." He spoke the words against Justin's ear. Justin spun in his arms and faced him. The shock and excitement couldn't be contained on his husband's expressive face. His heart did a little dance of joy just knowing he'd been the cause of the happiness.

"Like a time share?" Justin questioned.

"No, like a palace for my prince." He'd planned those words, but not Justin's reaction. Justin created distance between them by taking several steps back, that disbelieving look still plastered on his face.

"What?" Justin sounded unsure. Derek tucked his hands in his tuxedo pockets and remained quiet, letting Justin process his words. "How can we afford this?"

"You've always been uncomfortable with my wealth, so I don't talk about it, but I wanted to give this to you. Now that we're married, you have to accept my money, it's part of who I am, no matter how much you might not like that idea." Justin's eyes grew as big as saucers and his face flushed. Derek moved in closer; his honey hadn't taken a breath, and if he didn't soon, he would certainly pass out. "You have to sign the paperwork, but it's my gift to you for making me the happiest man in the world."

"I got you a watch," Justin pointed out, exhaling slowly.

"And I love that watch. It's my most prized possession." Justin had even engraved it with a Latin phrase—*Numquam tea mare desistam*—meaning I'll never stop loving you. He cherished that watch and never wanted to take it off. Justin remained in place as Derek edged toward him, pulling him into his arms once again. "Let's go check out the bedroom, the pictures online looked fantastic. Oh, and, babe, the best part…clothing's optional." Derek waggled his eyebrows. He figured he'd have Justin talked into skinny dipping in less than an hour. "And later, we can head down to the beach. If I remember correctly, someone once told me I'd look good wearing nothing but sand." He gave Justin a wink before leaning in and taking his lips in a playful kiss.

The End

BOOKS BY KINDLE ALEXANDER

What did you think of Closet Confession? Email us at kindle@kindlealexander.com. We would love to hear from you.

If you enjoyed Closet Confession, then you won't want to miss Kindle Alexander's bestselling novels:

Reservations

Painted On My Heart

Full Domain

Secret

Full Disclosure

Always

Double Full

The Current Between Us

Texas Pride

77251766R00078

Made in the USA
San Bernardino, CA
22 May 2018